PRAISE FOR JERUSHA AGEN

"Jerusha Agen once again delivers top-level suspense and thrilling action. *Covert Danger* kept me looking over my shoulder and flipping pages. Fast-paced suspense at its best."

DIANN MILLS, BESTSELLING AUTHOR OF *CONCRETE EVIDENCE*

Hidden Danger kept me reading and on the edge of my seat from page one through the end. Jerusha Agen writes a gripping suspense filled with danger, romance, and K-9s complete with a strong faith thread.

SHAREE STOVER, BESTSELLING AUTHOR OF *FRAMING THE MARSHALL*

"Fast-paced, explosive thriller. I couldn't turn the pages fast enough."

CARRIE STUART PARKS, AWARD-WINNING, BESTSELLING AUTHOR OF *RELATIVE SILENCE* ON *RISING DANGER*

RESCUED

BOOKS BY JERUSHA AGEN

GUARDIANS UNLEASHED

Midnight Clear (prequel novella)

Rising Danger (prequel)

Hidden Danger

Covert Danger

Unseen Danger

Lethal Danger

Terminal Danger

WINDY CITY WESTONS

Waylaid

Wasted (Fall 2025)

Watched (2026)

SECURITY LEAGUE

Protected (prequel novella)

Introverted (unnumbered novella)

Rescued

Trapped

SISTERS REDEEMED

If You Dance with Me

If You Light My Way

If You Rescue Me

SECURITY LEAGUE
BOOK ONE

RESCUED

JERUSHA AGEN

SDG Words, LLC

© 2025 by Jerusha Agen
Published by SDG Words, LLC
www.JerushaAgen.com

Library of Congress Control Number: 2025909335

ISBN 978-1-956683-50-9

Scripture quotations are from The ESV® Bible (The Holy Bible, English Standard Version®), copyright © 2001 by Crossway, a publishing ministry of Good News Publishers. Used by permission. All rights reserved.

This book is a work of fiction. Names, characters, places, and incidents are the product of the author's imagination or are used fictitiously. Any resemblance to actual events, locales, or persons, living or dead, is coincidental.

Soli Deo Gloria

Miami, Florida

THE SCREAMING blare sought her in the darkness.

A smoke detector?

The children.

The thought jolted Valena Greer upright in bed.

She blinked as the sound screeched again. An alarm, but not a smoke detector.

The lamp she'd left on illuminated the culprit on the nightstand—her phone. She grabbed the smartphone and pressed the button to silence the racket before it woke the children.

The screen flashed an alert in red. *SECURITY THREAT*.

Probably the raccoons again. They loved to climb over the fence this time of year and play with the security system the twins' father had insisted was necessary. Lance and his paranoia.

She set the phone to vibrate and lowered it back to the nightstand, but it trembled in her fingers. *A little sleep would be nice, raccoons.*

She slid out from under the covers and swung her legs over the side of the bed, the hardwood cool under her bare feet. Maybe she'd have to go out there and shoo the critters away. Or reset the security alarm. She yawned as she checked her phone.

The screen showed the view from one of Lance's security cameras. Looked like the one by the front door. No, the back door.

Something dark moved. A shadow. An outline of—

Were those people?

Her heart stopped.

Looked like two men, hovering by the door.

Lettering flashed at the bottom of the image: *SECURITY BREACH.*

She stared at the silhouettes, her jumpstarted heart pounding in her chest. This couldn't be happening. But it was.

The twins.

She launched off the bed and rushed into the hallway. Her hand automatically reached for the dimmer switch to turn up the lights, but she yanked back and kept moving. Brighter light would only make her more visible if the men got in.

She paused briefly to listen, peering over the railing at the entryway below.

Nothing. No one.

Had she imagined the shadows on the camera feed?

She went to the partially open door of the twins' room and quietly pushed it in.

Savannah and Sammy slept in their beds, just as she'd left them.

Her breathing calmed as she watched them. Plentiful nightlights gave the room a soft glow that clung to their blond hair and sun-kissed faces, making them look like the angels they were. They were so peaceful, their lives still untouched by anything that would undermine that.

She wouldn't scare them now over nothing. An incident like this could become a traumatic memory they didn't need.

She checked her phone again.

SECURITY BREACH still flashed, but the silhouettes were gone.

Maybe there hadn't been any in the first place. They could have been shadows cast by that bushy climbing vine on the outside wall. She probably hadn't been awake enough to make out what was actually there.

She looked at the twins. No, she wouldn't threaten their sense of security for no reason.

She slipped from the room, back into the hall.

The phone quaked against her palm.

She held her breath as she checked the screen.

UNAUTHORIZED ENTRY.

Her pulse stopped.

The men must be burglars.

She swung back into the twins' bedroom and shut the door.

The police would automatically be called now through the security system. They should be on their way. But how long would it take them to get there?

She had to protect the children.

The safe room. A manifestation of Lance's paranoia she'd never thought she would use. She was almost sorry for thinking he was nuts when he had shown her the upstairs access to the lower-level room.

How could she get the twins quietly and quickly down there? Sammy wouldn't wake up even if this were a bomb attack, so she'd have to carry him. She slipped her phone into the pocket of her cotton pajama shorts and went to Savannah's bed first, gently touching the two-year-old's shoulder.

"Savannah," she whispered. "Time to wake up, sweetie." Valena couldn't believe she was doing this on the first night Savannah was actually sleeping soundly in her grown-up bed.

Savannah's pink lips murmured something as she stirred.

"Come on, sweetie. You have to get up for me."

The girl's long lashes lifted, revealing the big blue eyes she shared with her brother. "Ena?" A smile curved her small mouth and clutched Valena's racing heart.

She couldn't let anything happen to her baby. Either of her babies. She smiled. "We're playing a special game. It's a pretend game." She helped Savannah sit up as she whispered. "We're going to pretend we're mice who have to be very quiet because we don't want the kitty to catch us. Okay?"

Her lashes stayed at half-mast as her mouth stretched in a yawn. "'Kay."

"Good girl." Valena lifted Savannah, relieved she didn't say anything more. The little girl was likely just too tired to chat as much as she usually did. With any luck, that would last until they could get to the safe room.

Valena carried Savannah to Sammy's bed and lowered her to the ground. "Remember, don't make a sound. Be a quiet mousy, okay?"

Savannah just swayed sleepily against Sammy's bed, her golden curls a fluffy halo around her head.

Valena scooped Sammy out from under the covers, her back muscles protesting with a twinge of pain at the angle. Seemed he grew bigger every night.

She shifted him to slump on her shoulder, his cheek hot against the skin left bare by her tank top. She took Savannah's hand and turned her around.

What if they were taking too long? Valena couldn't hear any sounds in the house, but her pulse thudded so loudly in her ears she might not be able to.

She took the kids to the walk-in closet, the motion-sensor light automatically illuminating the organized space.

A noise outside the room. A shuffle.

Her stomach dropped to her knees. She closed the closet door behind her, trying not to make a sound.

"Where are they?"

She held her breath at the male voice, tinged with a foreign accent. Spanish? She had to barricade the—

Her gaze fell on a metal beam and brackets fixed to the back of the door. Lance would think of something like that. She had never noticed since she hadn't closed the door from the inside. And never intended to.

She carefully, quietly slid the metal beam across the door. Her throat tightened as the beige walls started to push in around her.

"They're supposed to be here tonight. Try the other rooms. Watch out for the nanny."

She forced herself to focus on the voice in the bedroom instead of the nightmare of the shrinking space. What did the men expect to find? Jewels? There was no time to wonder. At least they were moving to a different room.

Where was that trap door Lance had shown her? By the wall?

She readjusted her hold on Sammy as she reached with her free hand to slide the shoe bin off the gray panel in the floor.

She grabbed the handle and pulled up the trap door.

A man's head emerged from the darkness.

CHAPTER
TWO

COOPER LEAPED out from the trap door opening, trying to reach the nanny before she could scream.

But the hand she clamped over her own mouth as she recoiled did the trick.

"Don't be scared. I'm a friend." He kept his voice at a whisper, not sure if the intruders had made it to the bedroom yet.

His gaze passed over the metal bar across the door. Good. The barricade would buy them time.

Savannah pointed a tiny finger at him. "Who—"

He grabbed her and covered her mouth to stop the rest of the sentence.

"Let her go." Valena stared at him with the fury of a mother bear about to attack, her hand protectively covering Sammy's head on her shoulder.

"I heard something." The man's Columbian-accented voice sounded close. In the bedroom.

Cooper took his hand off Savannah's mouth, but didn't put her down. They had to go. "I'm with Deacon Securities. We have to move."

He slipped through the trap door with the girl, his feet

finding the wooden stairs that descended to the basement. "Close the door behind you."

The sound of the nanny's steps registered as she followed, pausing only to close the door.

He continued down into the darkness.

The lights came on.

He jerked around.

Valena was just pulling her hand away from the switch.

"It's safer in the dark."

She shook her head, eyes big. "I'm not going down here if I can't see."

No time to argue, he continued down the staircase.

A banging sound echoed from above. They were breaking through the barricade.

He hit the cement floor of the unfinished basement and looked back.

Valena trailed close behind with Sammy, the boy somehow still sleeping in her arms. She reached the bottom of the stairs.

A slam. The trap door opening.

Valena turned back to look.

"What's that?" Savannah's question broke the silence like a crack of thunder.

"Down here!" The intruder's voice rocketed adrenaline through Cooper's veins.

He gripped Valena's elbow to get her attention. "Run."

He took off toward the dark hallway. Ran into the narrow passageway, Savannah jostling in his arms. His footsteps echoed too loudly on the cement floor, but speed was all that mattered now.

He paused at the end of the hall. Looked back.

Valena ran after him with Sammy.

Two taller heads bobbed behind her. The men were catching up.

"Hurry!" He dashed into the short passage on his left and went to the keypad by the steel door. He punched in the access code.

Valena reached his side just as the electronic door slid open.

"Get in."

She hesitated as he entered the safe room with Savannah.

Footsteps echoed in the passageway. Very close.

He grabbed the nanny's arm and pulled her inside.

"Hey!" The man's shout came as the door started to close.

Cooper set the girl down, ready to fight off the guy he glimpsed running to the shrinking opening.

The door shut. Sealed.

He let out a breath. But the adrenaline didn't stop.

This safe room wouldn't last ten minutes.

CHAPTER THREE

VALENA'S HEART rate caught up to her shallow breaths as she stood by Savannah in the middle of the small safe room. She squinted, waiting for her pupils to adjust to the brighter lighting.

But Savannah's eyes were huge. Scared.

Anger and grief stirred in Valena's belly as she pressed the girl against her leg. Savannah shouldn't have to feel this way. This shouldn't be happening. Valena narrowed her eyes at the tall stranger, his dark-haired head bent over his smartphone.

His knowledge of the safe room access code was evidence he actually was with Deacon Securities, the company Lance used for the security system. Lance had said he trusted the company. But the thought barely slowed her pulse or calmed her rising outrage.

The stranger tapped the screen. Was he calling the police?

She tilted her chin to better see his phone.

Movement. Some kind of video. At a time like this?

The security footage. He probably got the feed from the camera outside the safe room. She could, too. She pulled out her phone from the pocket of her pajama shorts.

A security breach alert flashed across the view from the camera that pointed at the safe room door.

Two men stood there. One of them kicked the door. The other fiddled with the keypad. Then they backed off and talked to each other. Too bad the camera didn't pick up sound.

They both looked up at the camera.

Her breath hitched.

They walked away.

Was that it?

"They're gone." She returned her phone to her pocket.

"No, ma'am." The stranger's answer made her start.

She'd barely realized she'd spoken her thoughts out loud. "How do you know that?"

He glanced up from his phone, his dark brown eyes and chiseled features much easier to see in the bright lighting of the safe room. His mouth angled upward, like a half-smile. But it dropped as he glanced back down at his phone.

Irritation sparked against her nerves. "So are we going to wait in here until the police arrive?"

"No, ma'am." His deep voice had a slight roughness that some women might find appealing. They'd also appreciate his muscular physique and broad shoulders that held the strap of a messenger bag, which crossed his toned chest and rested just behind trim hips. But she wasn't most women. He just rubbed her frustration the wrong direction.

Had he just said no? Heat, purely from annoyance, touched her cheeks as she registered his answer to her question. "Why wouldn't we wait for the police? That's the point of the safe room."

He looked at her again. "The men out there will make sure the police don't come."

"How could they do that?"

"It's a little complicated to explain at the moment."

"Ena." Savannah clutched Valena's leg with a tired whimper, interrupting the surge of irritation at his condescension.

"It's okay, sweetie. I'm here." Valena squatted down, ignoring the increasing soreness of the arm holding Sammy as she drew Savannah close to her other side. She tossed the watching stranger a glare. "You better try to explain it."

"Right now, my priority is to get the kids to safety. We only need the room to hold," he checked his wristwatch, "four more minutes."

She stood, indignation adding more heat to her face. "I'm their nanny. Keeping these children safe and happy is always my first priority." Just who did the man think he was?

The corner of his mouth twitched, and something too much like amusement sparkled in his eyes. "Good. Then you'll have no problem following me out."

"Out?"

"Yep. Our ride's almost here." He walked toward her.

She pulled Savannah with her to the side, but he went past them.

He reached up to the ceiling and unlatched an escape hatch she hadn't noticed before. The sculpted muscles of his upper arms bulged against the short black sleeves of his T-shirt as he tugged on something in the ceiling.

Not that she cared. She looked away. His physique and bearing told her all she needed to know. That, along with his trim haircut and love of giving orders. He had to be military. End of story.

Her gaze slid back to him just as he pulled down...a ladder?

Lance hadn't shown her that. Where did it lead? This place had more mysteries and passages than a haunted house. She'd felt better when she thought she knew about all of them.

The stranger's gaze rested on her. He couldn't be thinking—

"How do you expect to climb that with two children?" No way was she letting him try it.

"I brought equipment." He lifted the shoulder strap over his head and lowered the bag to the floor.

"Lance said if anything ever happened, we were supposed to stay in here until the police came."

The stranger squatted to remove what looked like harnesses from his bag. Did he even know who Lance was?

Fresh alarm renewed her suspicions about this mysterious character. "Why in the world would we follow *you* out of the safe room to who knows where?"

He abruptly stood and stepped close to her.

Her pulse sprinted, but he only held out his phone, the screen facing her. "Because they're going to get in here."

The camera feed showed the burglars, sparks flying from a torch they were using on the door.

"The kids can't be here when they do." He stepped away, letting her heartbeat attempt to slow down.

"Why would they want to get in here? Won't they just take the valuables and leave?"

"They aren't burglars." He picked up a harness from the floor.

"What—"

"I don't have time to answer your questions." He thrust a child-sized harness toward her. "Put this on Savannah."

He knew her name. Would Lance have told the security company his children's names?

"Hurry, will you? Or I can do it."

"No." Valena stepped between him and Savannah. She took the harness and turned to crouch in front of the little girl. "Hey, guess what, sweetie? We get to play dress up."

Savannah's face brightened with a smile that lit her blue eyes.

Valena never thought it would come in handy that

Savannah loved to try on any kind of clothing she could find. But her enthusiasm enabled Valena to help her get into the harness with one hand while still holding Sammy in her numbing right arm.

The stranger appeared next to her as soon as she finished.

"Hey, pretty girl." His velvety tone as he smiled at Savannah sent a shiver skipping along Valena's arms.

She stood, ignoring her odd response and watching closely as the man hooked a rope to Savannah's harness.

"How would you like to go for a piggy-back ride?" He squatted in front of her as he pulled the messenger bag strap over his head, onto his shoulder.

Savannah rewarded his sweet-talking with a giggle. She reached her little arms up toward him.

He laughed and turned around to let her climb onto his back.

Valena had to close her mouth after it dropped open. Savannah had only had two piggy-back rides in her life, and that was six months ago with Lance. But she had loved them.

The stranger stood and tied the rope attached to Savannah's harness around his waist, slipping his arm through the looped remainder of rope. He glanced at Valena. "I'll take her up and come back for Sammy."

Sammy. He knew Samuel had a nickname? She shoved her questions aside to make way for the more pressing priority. "I'll follow you with Samuel." No way was she going to let this stranger out of her sight with either of her babies.

The man looked at Sammy, still sleeping on her shoulder. "Will he stay like that?"

"I'll manage." She met his doubtful gaze without blinking.

"Fine." He turned toward the ladder. "Follow right behind me and hold him tightly. Let me know if you need help."

Valena barely held back a snort. Typical macho male,

thinking he could do everything while she couldn't do anything. The guy was definitely military.

"Squeeze against me, honey." Savannah obeyed his softened tone as he climbed the ladder through the square hatch opening.

Valena watched for a moment. She shouldn't follow him. Shouldn't have let him take Savannah out of what was probably the safest place for all of them.

But she could hear the buzzing of the torch cutting through the steel now. Louder couldn't be good.

She carefully switched Sammy to her left shoulder and started up the ladder. Tingles shot through her right arm as feeling returned. Changing arms might not have been such a great idea. She had to focus hard to make sure her numb, free hand gripped each rung of the ladder.

The passage the ladder cut through grew darker, and she couldn't see the end of it. What floor were they going to? She thought the stranger had meant out of the room. Had he meant out of the house? Up to the roof?

Savannah chatted the whole way, her musical tones too soft and distant for Valena to make out the words.

But she tried to focus on her baby's voice instead of the claustrophobic narrowness of the space and the darkness. Or the painful way the rungs of the ladder dug into her bare feet. At least no shoes probably helped her have better footing.

Her breathing grew more labored as her arms started to weaken, both the one she used for the ladder and the other under Sammy.

Something brushed her cheek. Spider webs? She shuddered.

Focus. She had to hang on for Sammy.

She could see her hand again. Had her eyes adjusted, or did that mean...?

She tilted her head back to look. Light. Cool-toned. Like moonlight. They really were headed for the rooftop. How could they escape from the burglars on the roof? Or maybe the plan was to hide where they would never think to look.

A rumbling noise reached her ears. No, more of a whirring. What in the world?

Savannah's voice drifted to her, but she couldn't make out the words as the other sound grew louder.

Valena was almost at the top, the whirring intense.

Her foot missed a rung, slipped.

She couldn't hang on.

Strong hands gripped under her arms, lifting her off the ladder and onto the roof in one quick motion.

She pulled away from the stranger. "I'm fi—" The reply died on her lips as she gaped at the source of the roaring noise behind him.

A helicopter stood on the roof, bathed in bright moonlight.

She'd known part of the roof was flat, but she hadn't realized it was large enough for a helicopter to use as a landing pad. Or that anyone would want to land one there.

"Come on!" The stranger's shout jolted her out of her confusion. He'd already moved close to the helicopter, dangerously near the rotating blades with Savannah still on his back. At least he stayed bent over as he beckoned for Valena to follow.

She glanced at the hole in the roof that was their escape from the safe room. The irony couldn't be missed. What was she doing blindly following this man with her babies?

Arm muscles screaming under Sammy's weight, she pulled out her cell phone.

The camera outside the safe room showed no one. And an open door.

"Move! Now!"

She jerked to see the yelling stranger gesturing wildly with his arms.

He looked somewhere behind her.

She turned that way.

The dark head of a man emerged from the opening above the ladder.

She took off, moving as fast as her tired legs could carry her and Sammy, fear driving her under the spinning blades and into the helicopter.

"Take the far seat!" The stranger gave her an unnecessary push as she climbed in and managed to crawl over the console to the far seat with Sammy.

A bearded man she didn't recognize sat in the pilot seat wearing a headset.

"Take off!"

The pilot nodded at the stranger's command.

The helicopter lifted off the ground as the stranger sat on the edge of the empty seat.

He pulled out a gun.

Alarm surged through Valena. He couldn't shoot with Savannah on his back. "What are you doing?" She shouted to be heard above the deafening noise of the helicopter.

The two burglars ran toward them. Carrying guns.

The stranger leaned toward the open door, lifting his Glock. If he dared to fall out or get Savannah hurt...

Valena reached for her.

"Stay back!" He didn't look behind to yell at her as he leveled his gun and shot at the men.

Savannah shrieked, and the burglars ducked, darting behind the chimney.

The helicopter rose higher, making Valena fall back into the seat, clutching Sammy tight.

The stranger finally closed the door, and the helicopter

tilted forward, sailing over rooftops and leaving the twins' home far behind.

Sammy raised his head, blinking sleepily.

If only Valena could wake up from this nightmare.

"WHAT DID you think you were doing?"

Cooper twisted in the co-pilot seat to better see Valena and hear her above the noise of the copter.

She held Savannah against her shoulder as the girl cried. Sammy sat in the seat beside her, straining to see out the window, though all he'd be able to glimpse would be city lights in the darkness below.

Valena's eyes flashed brighter than any city lights as she looked at him, clearly ready to defend her two cubs.

He'd known she was beautiful at surveillance distances. Didn't know she'd take his breath away at three feet. Those eyes. They were the color of the violets his mom grew in her garden.

"Are you going to answer me?"

He mentally shook off the hypnotic effect she seemed to have on him, even when she was furious enough to kill.

"How dare you risk a child's life with your little war games."

Ouch. The lady didn't pull any punches. "I can barely hear you." Though he'd heard her well enough to catch the insult.

"Will you put this on now?" He offered her the headset she'd already rejected once.

She snatched it from him and reached both arms around Savannah to put it on. Her chestnut hair bunched around the band on top of her head, making her look cute enough to take the edge off her low blow.

She positioned the mouthpiece deftly, as if she'd worn such an apparatus before.

He kept his tone even and calm as he spoke into his headset. "I was saving the kids' lives. And yours. You were all in much more danger if I had let them reach the copter."

Her narrow jaw tightened as she somehow kept her stroke on Savannah's hair gentle and steady. "Okay, Mr. Hero. Then you'll have no problem telling me who you are and where you're taking us."

He stifled a smile at her spunk. The lady backed up the fire in her eyes. No wonder Lance trusted her with his kids. "Cooper White. Deacon Securities."

One lovely eyebrow lifted. "You can't expect me to believe that. No security company rep would shoot at burglars and whisk us away in a helicopter." She bounced Savannah slightly in her arms without losing an ounce of the steel in her violet eyes. "Who are you really?"

He'd apparently have to give her some info. Enough to make her cooperate. "My name *is* Cooper White, but you're right, I'm not with Deacon Securities."

Something flashed in her gaze. Whether satisfaction or alarm, he couldn't be sure, since her suspicious expression didn't change.

"Lance created that company name so no one would be able to trace the source of his home security system. I'm actually the owner of Black and White Securities and Protection Agency, the real source behind Lance's security setup."

"Then why didn't you call the police when the alarm tripped?"

"This is beyond the scope of the police."

Her eyes narrowed. "You didn't want the police there for some reason, did you? Did you know those burglars?"

Wonderful. Now she had him pegged as a criminal. "I told you, those men were not burglars. That should be obvious, given how they pursued the kids all over the house and onto the roof."

Her brown eyebrows dipped as she muttered something he couldn't make out.

"I'll explain everything when we land, okay? I just need you to trust me."

"I don't know you, and you've already lied to me once. Why would I trust you?" She stroked Savannah's small back and reached to touch Sammy's head, though the boy was fine.

Looked like he'd have to use some more ammo. He had to get her on his side by the time they landed, or she'd slow them down, at best. Worst case scenario, he might have to do something drastic he did not want to do.

He pulled the photo of himself and Lance out of his jeans' pocket. Here was hoping it would do the trick. He extended the picture toward her.

She looked from it to his face, then snapped the photo from his fingers as if afraid he might grab her.

"We'll land in thirty minutes."

Her gaze jumped to his. "Thirty minutes? I thought we were going to the police." She clutched Savannah closer.

Sammy leaned into her side and started to whimper, seemingly out of nowhere. Probably picked up on Valena's tension.

His gut twisted. He didn't want to scare any of them.

"Where are you taking us?" Protective anger cinched her voice.

But the less she knew the better for her and the children.

"We're going somewhere safe. This is about a lot more than a break-in."

Her violet eyes searched his face, doing odd things to his pulse.

"You need to trust me. This is to keep the kids safe." He reached over and tapped the photo in her hand that she'd barely looked at. "He's a friend. That has to be enough for now."

Valena caressed Sammy's silky hair as he drifted off, his head on her lap while his body stretched onto the other seat. Savannah had gone to sleep a few minutes before, her tears still damp on Valena's shoulder. Both kids asleep, just in time to be awakened again as they landed.

She tilted her chin to catch the view out the window.

Lights formed a lopsided x-shape on the black ground below. Runways at an airport? Looked like it was in the middle of nowhere. She could only glimpse a smattering of other lights, indicating a small number of houses or buildings a long way from the airport. If it was an airport.

Everything looked so different from the air. Maybe the city was bigger than it appeared.

The pilot said something to Cooper, and the helicopter started to descend.

Her heart rate picked up speed, muscles tensing as she started to visualize a plan. The breath she'd barely let go in the last thirty minutes locked in her throat as the helicopter lowered closer to those lights.

If this lunatic thought she was going to let him kidnap her and the twins without a fight, he had no idea who he was dealing with.

She glanced at the supposed hero. White teeth flashed as

he chatted with the pilot, talking about something she couldn't hear since she'd taken off her headset when he kept ignoring her. Didn't matter. Leaving them to their own conversation kept them distracted and gave her the advantage of surprise.

Cooper White, or whatever his real name was, had the upper hand on the helicopter. She couldn't exactly jump from the air with twin two-year-olds.

But on the ground, they'd be even.

He turned his head, dark eyes catching her stare. Was that a twinkle?

She looked away. She wasn't so easy to distract. He'd have to try a different tactic than charm if he wanted to get the edge on her.

The man was clearly an adventure junky and ex-military. Positively not her type. No matter how cute he was.

"I guess kids can sleep through anything." He raised his voice to be heard over the noise.

She refused to acknowledge his friendly act with even a glance. She readjusted her hold on Savannah, the girl's head nestling farther into Valena's neck.

She glanced out the window. Her heart skipped a beat at the proximity of the ground. What was she going to do with the twins in the middle of nowhere? How could she get them away from the man and somewhere safe? She needed more information, to begin with.

Cooper was facing the front again.

She reached for the headset where she'd laid it next to Sammy. She quickly put it on, trying not to jostle Savannah. "Where are we?"

If Cooper was startled to suddenly hear her voice in his headset, he didn't show it. He merely sent her a glance. "Lake Wales."

Not completely the middle of nowhere, but close. At least

he wasn't trying to hide the location from her. That was a good sign. She could try to reason with him one more time. She moistened her lips. "Why are we in the middle of the state? The twins need to get home."

He shook his head. "It's not safe."

"Okay, then we go to the police."

Cooper looked forward as the helicopter touched down, jostling the twins.

Should she escape with them now? While he was still in the front seat? She could never gather up both twins quickly enough. She'd have to play along until she was already holding them and on her feet.

She removed her headset and worked to unbuckle her seatbelt that was partially under Sammy's head.

Cooper talked to the pilot as the pounding whir slowly decreased, letting her catch the tail end of their conversation. "...right. Thanks, man." Cooper patted the pilot on the shoulder like he was an old pal.

"So you're good with the plane?" The pilot glanced over his shoulder.

Cooper nodded. "Yeah, I've got it. We'll get out of here in ten."

Alarm spurred her heart rate even faster. "What plane?"

Cooper removed his headset as he glanced at her, then looked back at the pilot. "Give us a few minutes?"

"I need to refuel and stretch my legs anyway." The pilot opened his door.

"Keep your eyes open, will you?"

The pilot nodded, as if he was in on Cooper's secret, and exited the helicopter.

Good. Now she only had one man to escape. She abandoned getting her question about the plane answered. Whatever his plan was, she wasn't going along with it anyway.

She touched Sammy's shoulder and gently shook it. "Time to get up, Sammy."

"Might be better if he stays asleep. We have a long trip ahead of us yet."

She glared at Cooper. "You've got to be kidding me. There's a legal term for what you're doing. It's called trafficking."

His deep laugh hit the walls of the helicopter.

She stared.

His smile faded as he looked at her. "Sorry. I shouldn't laugh. I just...nothing could be further from the truth." He held out his hands. "I'm protecting the kids. That's what you said you want, too."

She shook her head. "Not good enough." She pulled the photo out from under Sammy's shoulder and held it up. "And some picture isn't going to convince me of anything. There's only one reason a guy your age would carry around a printed photo like this instead of on your phone. To con someone." She let the snapshot drop to the floor. "Well, I don't make for an easy mark."

She caught the glint in his eyes before he could hide it. She'd called his bluff. Checkmate.

But he didn't look as rattled as she'd like. "Okay. You're right. I did bring that picture along for your sake because I knew you'd only trust me if you knew I was Lance's friend." He picked up the photo from the floor. "This picture is very real. Taken when we both worked at the same place."

Yeah, right. "You don't expect me to believe you're a doctor, too."

He didn't blink. "I used to be an agent with the DEA."

She stared at him, looking for a sparkle of humor or the glance away that signaled a lie. "The DEA. As in the Drug Enforcement Administration?"

He nodded.

Could he be telling the truth? Even if he was, it didn't make sense of anything. "What does that have to do with Lance?"

"Lance is not a doctor, and he's not with the W.H.O."

A DISBELIEVING CHUCKLE escaped Valena's lips. "What?" She stared at Cooper as if he was the biggest liar she'd ever met.

Savannah shifted, pulled back from Valena's chest, and rubbed her eyes with little fists.

Valena glared past her to Cooper. "I've worked for Lance for two years. I live in the family's house. I know him way too well to fall for whatever it is you're up to."

Cooper blew out a breath and ran his hand over his hair. "Lance said you wouldn't be easy to convince if I had to extract the twins."

Her eyes narrowed. "If you mean easy to fool, you're right."

Admiration mixed with frustration as he bit back a retort. Lance hadn't been kidding when he'd called her smart and tough. She wasn't going to let anything threaten those kids. Except the danger she couldn't see coming.

She shook Sammy again, a little harder this time. "Come on, baby. We have to go."

The boy murmured and slowly sat up in the other seat.

She was going to bolt. Her tense posture and insistence on

waking Sammy when she didn't want to get on the plane screamed she was hatching a plan.

Cooper's stomach clenched. If she tried to run with the kids, he'd have to stop her by force. And ruin any chance of gaining her cooperation and trust.

She threw him a glance. "If you're really a friend, you'll take us back to Miami right now. Or at least let us go so I can get the kids home."

A last ditch effort to get her way. But he couldn't give her what she wanted. "I can't do that."

She stiffened. "You won't let us go?"

"You're making this sound like a kidnapping." Frustration tightened his tone.

"That's what most courts would call snatching people out of their home in the middle of the night."

They didn't have time for this. He gripped his knees to keep from grabbing the kids to speed things up. "I don't recall any snatching."

"Oh, that's right. We went voluntarily because you convinced me the burglars were going to…what was it they were going to do exactly?" She reached for the door and pushed it open, holding Savannah with one arm.

At least she was starting to move. "We can continue this conversation while we load the kids on the plane." He dropped out the front passenger door before she could respond and rounded the nose of the copter.

He opened the door by Sammy, revealing Valena's flashing eyes.

"While we *what*?"

He reached for Sammy.

She blocked him with her arm. "Don't touch him."

Cooper held up his hands to signal surrender.

"We're not going anywhere else with you. You haven't

given me one reason to believe anything you've said, which, by the way, doesn't make any sense."

"Fine, you want the whole story?" His voice rose to match her heightened volume. "Lance is a special agent with the DEA." Cooper pulled out his cell from his pocket and brought up Lance's last text message. "He went off grid in Columbia and the last thing anyone heard from him is this." Cooper held up the phone, screen facing her.

She would see Lance's name as the sender ID and the short text: *Code Violet*.

"That's it?" Her eyebrows lifted.

"What do you mean, that's it?" He shoved the phone into his back pocket. That still didn't make a dent?

"That's not Lance's number, and I have no idea what that code thing is supposed to mean."

Cooper gripped the doorframe. "Lance did not tell me you would be so incredibly exasperating."

She gave him a sardonic chuckle. "Oh, nice. Lance didn't tell *me* anything about you."

She reached for Sammy. "It's okay, baby. We're going home."

The boy responded to her softened tone, reaching out his arms, and she hefted him to her left side.

Cooper jogged around the copter again before she could exit the open door on the other side. He got there just as she was about to step out with her full load of both twins.

"I can take one." He reached to help, but her glare stopped him.

She managed to step down on her own, but tipped off-balance from the uneven weight of the kids.

Cooper put his hand on her arm to keep her from pitching over.

She pulled away, her gaze scanning the moon-bathed

airfield. Her attention stopped on the main building five hundred feet away, its lights like torches in the darkness.

She was going to run.

"Before you try to take off..."

Those violet eyes angled to Cooper. Wary and ready. Like the eyes of a cornered cat preparing to fight.

He needed to defuse the situation, fast. "Maybe we can start over." He tried a smile. "I'm Cooper White. I'd offer a handshake, but you've got your hands full already."

She tipped her chin, eyes narrowing. "We're not going to be friends."

"I can see that." A grin tugged his mouth at the sight she made. A child in each arm, standing barefoot in her pajamas, and yet she bore the confidence of a soldier with the upper hand. The woman was amazing. "Code Violet is you."

She blinked at him. "Me?"

"Yeah. Well, the kids really, but we knew you were part of the package."

"The package?"

His smile dropped as he sighed. "I'm not saying this right. Lance hired me, Black and White Agency, to watch out for you and the kids if anything happened to him."

She pressed her lips together. She had to know how much Lance cared about safety. It fit he would hire Cooper on top of the home security system.

"Okay." She leveled a challenging gaze at him. "Prove it."

Movement behind her caught Cooper's eye. Headlights. Coming this way.

They were out of time.

CHAPTER
SIX

"IS THAT—"

"We have to go. Now." Cooper gripped Valena's arms with a gentle but firm hold and captured her gaze in his. "I've been watching you and the kids the last six months because Lance asked me to."

He spoke quickly, urgency punching every word. "He was scared people might come after his kids to get at him. You may not believe me, but I know you're smart, and you love these kids more than anything. Right now, we have to get them on the plane and take off before that vehicle reaches us. Or the twins will be in danger."

Was he telling the truth? What if she went with him and it turned out he was some psyc—

"Please," his usual commanding tone frayed with a thread of concern she could almost buy, "trust me a little longer, and I'll get you the proof you want."

She had no solid reason to trust him. But she saw only truth and sincerity in those rich brown eyes that looked deeply into hers. If he was making all this up, he had to have some reason. And he hadn't actually forced her to do anything. If his intentions were bad, wouldn't he have already tried to drag her onto the plane or take the twins from her?

Instead, he stood there reasoning, almost pleading with her.

His gaze sprang away, probably to the approaching lights behind her, then jumped back to her face, a fierce black shadow moving into his eyes. "We have to go."

One test. "You weren't DEA. You were Army."

"I was both." He didn't miss a beat. No shifting gaze. No denial.

Her gut said he was telling the truth. "We'll go with you."

"Hallelujah." He grabbed Sammy from her arms before she could blink and took off at a sprint. "Hurry!"

She jogged to follow him past the nose of the helicopter.

A plane waited about sixty feet away on the tarmac—a small, private plane, but a little bigger than the others she'd seen tied down.

She glanced to the south as she hustled after him.

The lights moved closer. Clearly headlights now, from what looked like an SUV. Who was in it? The burglars couldn't have made it that far so quickly on land.

Savannah whimpered, probably because of the jostling.

Valena slowed to a walk, only ten feet from the plane. "Sweetie, it's okay. We're okay." Her insides twisted at what this experience might be doing to the twins. What trauma was this memory going to create in their lives?

Cooper had already put Sammy in one of the back seats. He reached to take Savannah, but Valena pulled her away.

"I can take her." She climbed in with Savannah before he could argue.

"Strap the kids in and yourself, too." He shut the door hard.

Always ordering. Good thing for him she would want to buckle the twins in anyway.

She checked for a pilot, but the front seat was empty.

Cooper opened the door and hopped into that seat himself. He knew how to fly?

"It's going to be tight." He didn't look back as he started the plane.

She looked out the window over Sammy.

The dark SUV was getting close, driving along roads that must wind around to the runway.

"What that?" Sammy squirmed to see out the window as she tried to buckle him in.

The plane started to move, and she abandoned the effort, scooping him up and holding him on her lap instead. At least Savannah had cooperated and was quietly sitting with her seatbelt on.

"No. Down." Sammy struggled and whined in her lap. He needed sleep, not flying in a plane in the middle of the night.

Cooper taxied the plane to the runway.

She watched for the SUV out the window.

It raced alongside them on a parallel road. Then it turned, veered off the pavement onto the grass. Angled to intersect them.

"Watch out!" She instinctively shouted the warning.

Cooper lifted the plane off the ground.

The SUV soon became a shrinking dot that disappeared in the darkness below.

The twins shrieked, Savannah crying as she grabbed her ears.

"Oh, sweetie, it's okay." They'd never felt the rapid change in air pressure before. Valena tried to comfort both children at once, Savannah too far away to hug with her seatbelt on.

Helplessness clogged Valena's throat, souring the taste of anger already in her mouth. Cooper better have told her the truth.

A horrible thought threatened her sanity. What if the good

guys were in that SUV instead of on this plane? It could've been the FBI trying to rescue her and the twins from their kidnapper, and she'd played right into his hands.

She tried to swallow. What if she'd just made the worst mistake of her life?

Looking at her crying, unhappy babies, her heart squeezed. She wouldn't be the only one to suffer.

Cooper turned his head to check on his precious cargo since he hadn't heard a peep for the last ten minutes.

The twins curled up together on the seat next to Valena, their small bodies wrapped in blankets like caterpillars sharing a cocoon.

The tension in his shoulders relaxed a little at the sight. It had taken half an hour for them to calm down. But they were safe and happy now. Thank the Lord for the resilience of children. *And thank You, Lord, that Valena let them get on this plane.*

The silent prayer came naturally, yet stuck out like a flower in a snowdrift. Probably the first time he'd prayed in months. Guilt triggered with the thought.

"We're worried about you, son." The statement from Cooper's dad in their last phone conversation reverberated in his memory. And his mom's much more direct question, *"Why don't you go to church anymore?"*

Valena's voice interrupted the replay.

He glanced back to see her watching him as if waiting for an answer to a question. "I can't hear." Very true this time, though the plane noise wasn't as deafening as the helicopter. He waved her to the front, indicating the co-pilot's seat.

She slipped into the spot next to him, her slight body making the seat look grossly oversized.

He handed her the other headset, which she took without argument.

He smiled when she had it on. "Nice job calming the kids."

She folded her arms across her dark purple tank top, staring straight out at the night sky.

Right. They weren't going to be friends. But he could still be friendly. "I think there should be another blanket back there if you want it." He thumbed over his shoulder.

She sent him a glare.

At least he got her to look at him. That was progress. Even if he'd irked her again. He glanced at the clock. *3:47 a.m.* "I suppose this is when they're usually in bed anyway, huh?"

She pressed her lips together.

Still not talking to him.

"Of course it is, and that's where they should be now. At home. In bed."

Make that talking. Definitely talking.

She turned flashing violet eyes on him. "I'm ready for that convincing explanation now."

He held back a sigh. He couldn't tell her as much as she'd want to know. She didn't need to know things that would frighten her and put her in more danger. He fiddled with the instruments to buy some time to pick the safest information.

"Let's start with where we're going."

Good. An easy one. "Wisconsin."

"What?" Her voice shot into a high register next door to a squeak.

Maybe not so easy. He kept his gaze ahead and his tone even. "That's why I'm thinking you might want to reconsider using a blanket."

"The weather is the least of my concerns at the moment. What right do you think you have to take me and the children off to Wisconsin in the middle of the night?"

He bit his tongue to keep from asking if the middle of the

day would've been fine. "Why don't we try to stay calm? We don't want to wake the kids."

"We?"

He glanced at her in time to catch the color of her face change to angry red.

"You don't have a clue what's best for them." She pushed out the words through clenched teeth. "The most important thing right now is finding out just what their kidnapper has in mind."

"I'm not a kidnapper." He fought down the irritation she always seemed to stir in him. "We're going to a place Lance has in Wisconsin."

"He never told me he had a house there."

Cooper met her suspicious gaze. "You're going to have to get used to the idea that there are a lot of things Lance never told you."

She turned her head away, the smooth curve of her jaw tightening.

"He had the cottage in case he or his family needed to hide away."

"Why would they have to hide? Lance is normal. His wife was normal. Rich, sure, but they don't need a safe house across the country." Doubt and skepticism laced her tone.

"I don't know what you think of as normal, but I've already told you Lance isn't exactly who you think. He's—"

"DEA?" She shifted sideways in the seat toward him. "You really expect me to believe that?"

"I said I would give you proof."

"And I still don't see any."

"Not on the plane. At the cottage."

"Cottage. In Wisconsin."

He felt her stare as he checked the gauges on the instrument panel.

"That's convenient. Let me guess, it's waaay out in the north woods?"

He obviously couldn't answer that question truthfully at the moment. This was all clearly coming off much more creepy than protective from her point of view. He wracked his brain for something that would make her trust him, at least long enough to get her to the cottage. Lance had said she'd be tough, but Cooper hadn't expected the Great Wall of China.

If he didn't come up with something convincing, she was going to bolt as soon as they hit the tarmac. He'd never get her to the cottage, or at least not without the kind of tactics he didn't want to use. But his first responsibility was to Lance's kids. If she interfered with that, put them in danger even out of good intentions, he would have to use force whether he wanted to or not.

He had to show he was a friend. Or at least that he was a good guy. "Ask me anything."

Her eyebrows stretched to her forehead.

Too late, he realized that was too wide open. He scrambled to prevent the offer from blowing up in his face. "Ask me anything about Lance or the kids. Something I'd only know if I really knew Lance and his family."

"Okay." She paused, probably thinking of the toughest questions she could. "What was Miriam's maiden name?"

"Lawrence."

"When did she die?"

He knew the date, but too many details could make it look like he'd memorized a facts sheet. He went with vaguer. "One year ago."

She narrowed her eyes.

Too vague. "Thirteen months. December fourteenth. Died of pancreatic cancer."

Surprise registered in her gaze. But he was sure she wasn't

done. So far, she'd only asked him things anyone could find out.

"When did Miriam hire me?"

"When the twins were one month old." She wanted information, he'd give it to her. "Seven months after you graduated from college with two degrees in physics and biochemistry. I've always been curious, why didn't you get a job more in your field?"

"None of your business. And if that's supposed to snow me under, it didn't work. Any clever kidnapper could've researched all of that."

He grinned. "Well, at least you think I'm clever."

There was less challenge in the gaze she rested on him, as if she might be having some doubts about her kidnapping theory. Was he finally winning her over?

"If Lance is working for the DEA like you say, then where is he? What is he doing?"

"That, I can't answer."

"Why am I not surprised?" Distrust slid back into her eyes, along with the intention to run as soon as she got the chance.

He needed some evidence that he knew more than the external facts. "Did Lance ever tell you about his honeymoon with Miriam?"

"No."

So much for that idea.

"Miriam did."

Hope sparked in his chest. "Did she tell you about the place they stayed in by a lake?" He glanced over to catch her nod. "They went out in a rowboat to fish, and Lance managed to fall in." Cooper smiled. Lance had laughed so hard when he'd told the story.

Valena watched Cooper, her face devoid of reaction.

"Miriam said it looked like she'd have to be the one to put the meat on the table—"

"—in this marriage," Valena finished with him.

"The cottage we're going to now is the place in the story—their honeymoon getaway."

Decision banished the doubt in her eyes. Got her.

Northern Wisconsin

COOPER CHECKED the rearview mirror as he navigated the road that was covered with snow and ice packed down by tires. Apparently, the snowplow crews had decided drivers could clear the rest of the remote road themselves.

No sign of a tail in the growing light from the morning sun. At least this leg of the trip was going according to plan. The pre-paid rental car had been waiting at the air strip as he'd planned, complete with car seats for the kids.

But Valena seemed far from impressed.

He looked at her in the reflection of the mirror.

She sat in the back seat between the kids, lips pressed tightly together as she held the icy silence she'd maintained since he'd told her they couldn't risk stopping for diapers.

They had come in without a tail. He couldn't jeopardize the kids' safety by being spotted along the route to the cottage. Though the more that awful stench filled the car, the more his own resolve wavered. Two hours on the plane with crying kids and smelly, dirty diapers had made him wish a hundred times he'd thought to bring diapers on the flight.

A cry started up in the back. Savannah.

"We need to stop."

Here they went again. Cooper braced himself for another argument.

"Savannah's uncomfortable, and I'm worried about diaper rash." Valena murmured something to the girl in softer tones. She had managed to get Savannah to sleep again on the plane —she could probably do the same thing again.

"I'm sorry she's uncomfortable, but you have to trust me on this. If we stop, we're likely to be seen. If we leave a trail, we'll make it easy for...the wrong people to find us. Believe me, you don't want to risk the kids like that." A little discomfort wasn't worth the child's life. Or any of their lives.

"I'll tell you what I do and don't want, all right? My priority is the children, and I understand their needs a whole lot better than you do." Her voice trembled on the last word, contradicting the steel in her tone.

He glanced in the rearview mirror to catch her shivering. "Are you cold?"

"I'm fine." She crossed her arms, but the second shiver that wracked her body couldn't be hidden so easily. Nor could the blue color of her lips that he hadn't noticed when it was darker.

Idiot. He should've made her use the other blanket he'd grabbed from the plane in the rush to get in the car without being spotted. But she'd double-wrapped Savannah instead.

He was cold, too, but a T-shirt and jeans provided a lot more warmth than the tank and shorts she wore.

The digital thermometer in the car reported the outdoor temp to be twenty-one degrees Fahrenheit. The jump from Florida to Wisconsin winter was no joke.

He turned up the setting for the heater. "Are you getting heat back there?"

"Look." She leaned forward to point out the windshield. "There's a shop at that station. I bet they sell diapers."

He looked where she indicated.

A much larger gas station than he'd have expected out there stood at the top of a hill.

He shook his head. "We can't stop. It's too dangerous."

"You know what's dangerous?" She leaned close enough to the front seats that he could feel the blazing heat from her eyes. "Letting a stranger take us to some unknown location in the Wisconsin wilderness. I've had enough. You either pull into this gas station, or I will assume you care nothing for these children and act accordingly."

The gas station came up on the right, but he firmed his jaw and drove past. She'd have to learn to trust him. But he wouldn't risk the kids' safety to buy it.

"Fine."

He checked in the mirror to see what she was up to.

"I'm calling the police." She held up...her phone?

Triple idiot. He'd forgotten she had it with her. And probably hadn't turned off the GPS.

She started dialing. Only took a second to dial 911. And they'd be blown.

He braked. Harder than he should've for the kids. The twinge of guilt was swallowed by frustration as he swung the car into a U-turn. "Tell me you turned off the GPS on your phone." He ground out the words, not sure whether to be angry with her or himself for not having taken the device earlier.

"It's always off."

Relief loosened half the tension pinching his neck muscles. That should slow down one of their tails, at any rate. "Could still be traced." He muttered the words as he pulled into the empty parking lot of the gas station.

"Only by a government agency. And that's not a problem, is it?" She cocked an eyebrow at him.

He looked away from her reflection, ignoring the probe. "My phone is secure, but we'll have to get rid of yours." All the players in this game could eventually get her location data as long as she had that phone. He put the car in park next to a mountain of snow that must have accumulated over months of plowing the parking lot. He twisted around to face her. "We can get you a burner phone."

She stared at him like an agent about to be disarmed, those lovely eyes full of shock and defensive anger.

He was not getting her phone without a fight. Great. "We'll stick with just keeping the location tracking turned off for now. But don't use it for anything."

She set the phone on the seat beside her, no nod or agreement.

He had to make sure they didn't pick up a tail thanks to her cell. But he didn't want to force her to give it up. One look at the intensity in her gaze and her rigid posture between shivers told him she'd run or do something equally dangerous if he made her feel cornered. He had to risk giving her a little breathing room. For the moment.

She gripped the door handle, then paused. Maybe rethinking what she was wearing?

"I'll get the diapers so you can stay with the kids." And letting her walk inside in her pajamas would attract way too much attention. He'd had a hard enough time keeping his own eyes and mind in line.

She launched into a description of the types and sizes of diapers he should buy and which ones not to buy that made his head spin more than foreign language training in Special Forces.

He watched a navy blue sedan as it pulled into the parking lot and stopped at a gas pump. He nodded when she ended the list of instructions. "Got it." Diapers for two-year-olds. Some package had to just say that.

Her skeptical eyebrows signaled he must have let his confusion show more than he should've, but he didn't have time to calm her doubts. They'd sat there too long already.

A heavyset, middle-aged man got out of the car that appeared to hold a woman and possibly a child in the back seat. Still no other people in sight.

He put his hand on the keys in the ignition. The car might get a little cold if he took them, but with Valena's mistrust of him, he couldn't risk leaving her with an easy getaway option. "Keep the doors locked while I'm gone." He turned off the engine and took the keys. "No matter what happens."

He glanced back before opening the door.

Her violet eyes held a storm of questions and frustration.

For the sake of the kids, he hoped she listened.

More orders. Valena shivered as she watched Cooper cross the parking lot, trying not to dwell on his confident stride and sculpted build. She didn't miss how he subtly scanned his surroundings the whole way.

She rolled her eyes. Carbon copy of her father. As if a gas station in the middle of Wisconsin was a middle-eastern war zone.

She jumped at a tapping sound. Jerked to look at the window

Nothing was there. Just the man fifty feet away, pumping gas into his car.

She blew out a sigh. Now she was doing it.

"No matter what happens."

He'd probably said that just to scare her.

Another shiver shook her body, and she wrapped her cold arms around herself.

Savannah's whine turned into a cry.

Valena pushed aside her irritation to focus on the little girl's needs.She unbuckled Savannah from the car seat and transferred the girl to her lap. Valena's heart rate calmed as she held Savannah's warm body close, the scent of shampoo from the girl's soft curls soothing her frayed nerves.

"Eat me?" Sammy tried to squirm out of his straps.

"Not right now. We'll get breakfast soon. Look at that big mountain right there." She pointed Sammy's attention to the gigantic pile of snow.

Irritation sparked to life again. She should've told Cooper to get food and something to drink, too. He'd distracted her from what mattered with his nonsense about the phone.

She woke up her cell to check the screen. No answer to the text she'd sent Lance while Cooper had tied down the plane at the airstrip.

She hadn't been about to admit to Cooper that she'd already used her phone. She would use it more, too, if Lance texted her back.

Cooper had almost had her with his story about Lance and Miriam. He could have only known that if he did truly know Lance. Both Lance and Miriam were private people who didn't share personal information until they knew a person very well.

But the probability that Cooper had told the truth about knowing Lance didn't mean she had to believe his whole story. The idea of Lance being an agent for the DEA was insane. Maybe Cooper was a friend of Lance's who'd gone off the deep end or something. Friends sometimes turned on friends. She vaguely remembered reading once that kidnappings were often pulled off by someone close to the family.

Yet the theory of Cooper being a kidnapper didn't feel quite likely either. There was something about him, more than his good looks and charm. In all his attempts to be friendly, he'd never looked at her wrong, even though she was in her lightweight pajamas. He wasn't harsh with the twins, at least so far. He hadn't tried to force Valena to go with him at the airport. A kidnapper wouldn't be quite such a...gentleman, would he?

The diaper situation was bad, though. His callous attitude about the twins' discomfort proved him to be at least another clueless male who wanted nothing to do with children. She couldn't trust a man like that on a trek into the wilderness with her babies.

She needed an answer from Lance. She looked at her phone.

Nothing.

She'd never had to use his emergency number before. He didn't like to be contacted when he was gone, so she would always wait for his occasional calls to check in.

But this situation definitely qualified as an emergency.

She only hoped he would answer before her phone's battery died.

The battery symbol indicated it was half gone already.

Maybe she should use the phone to call the police before it was too late.

"What that?" Sammy still stared at the snowy mountain.

"That's snow." Which the twins had never seen. And she certainly hadn't planned to teach them about it with a sudden trip to the Midwest.

"Why?"

"Snow is cold, white stuff that falls from the sky."

This was insane. She was in the middle of nowhere in freezing Wisconsin with two-year-old twins and a guy who could very well be a lunatic, luring her into a winter wasteland to do her in and...

No. She closed her eyes, forced a deep breath, and stroked

Savannah's hair back from her face. Panicking with wild imaginings of what could happen to the twins would not help. She needed to stay calm and rational. Use her head.

If only Lance had made a habit of checking in at regular intervals like she'd practically begged him to do. The kids needed stability in their lives. That's where security came from. She could structure and schedule every other second of every day, but Lance always had to be the big unknown.

He could go weeks, eight weeks one time, without checking in. Longer without wanting to video chat with his own children. And it was always random and unscheduled when she did hear from him. At least he tried to call at a reasonable hour, even when it was nighttime at his location.

Or so he had said.

But did she really know? Was he ever where she had thought? If Cooper was telling the truth, Lance had never been doing what he had told her he was.

Her mind raced. If he worked for the DEA, what else was a lie? Had Miriam known? What if she hadn't been a doctor either?

Valena shook her head to banish the thought. She would not believe ill of her deceased friend. A year of caring for Miriam's kids and living in the same house while she was alive had convinced Valena of the woman's authenticity and genuine love for her family. The idea that Lance might have lied to her about his life, too, churned Valena's stomach.

He hadn't traveled so much when Miriam was alive, but even then he had hardly ever made it home for dinner. He hadn't worked with the W.H.O. then. Or at least, he had said he was working at a hospital in the ER. He had cited crazy hours and unexpected emergencies that made him stay out all night sometimes.

Valena was a nanny, not a marriage counselor, so she had never talked to Miriam about the problem. Miriam herself worked long hours as a doctor, too. At least that's what she had said.

This was crazy. Thanks to Cooper, Valena was starting to doubt the truth of everything except Cooper himself. Wasn't that how the best conmen worked? She needed to have a backup plan if her fears about him proved justified.

She kept one arm wrapped around Savannah while she searched the Internet on her phone for the town name proclaimed by the water tower a few miles back.

Within a couple of minutes, she'd gotten her bearings and figured out where they were. Farther north than she'd thought. Her dad had been based about two hundred miles from there during a six-month stint when she was thirteen.

Her next search results brought up the number and location of the nearest police station. Should she call them?

Something thudded against the window.

She swung to look.

A man watched her.

CHAPTER
EIGHT

HER HEART STOPPED.

The man in the striped winter hat grinned and waved a gloved hand close to the window.

"Can I help you?" Though muffled, Valena instantly recognized Cooper's voice behind the stranger who had been at the gas pump before.

Her breath returned as the man straightened and turned away.

She twisted to see Cooper through the back window.

Shopping bags sat at his feet on the blacktop. His hands hung loosely at his sides, as if he were relaxed.

Her gaze went to the holster at his hip.

The strap over the gun was unsnapped.

"Yeah." The man walked closer to Cooper but stopped at a safe distance. Maybe he'd seen the holster, too. "Do you know how to get to the Strawberry Inn from here?"

Valena's pulse started to slow as the tension slid from her muscles. Just a normal person asking for directions. That was all. Thanks to Cooper, she'd nearly had a heart attack.

"No clue." Cooper's tone packed just enough civility and

warning to send the man away quickly. "Why don't you ask inside?"

"Good idea." The man headed that direction, giving Cooper a wide berth. "Thanks."

"Don't mention it." He waited as the man veered to his car by the gas pump and got in it. Cooper then finally picked up the bags and walked around to the driver's side. He opened the door, letting in a blast of frigid air.

"Will you start the car? It's freezing in here."

He blinked at her greeting, but slid into the seat and did as she asked.

What'd he expect? A hero's welcome? He was the one who was imagining danger where there wasn't any and trying to make her just as paranoid.

He thrust a package of diapers toward her.

She looked at the label instead of staring at his dark eyes that glittered, moist from the cold wind. The diapers were Sammy's size. She gave Cooper a frown. "Why didn't you get two sizes?"

"They didn't have Savannah's size."

"But Samuel's a size bigger."

His T-shirt stretched over his broad shoulders as he lifted them in a shrug. "Best I could do."

She let out a sigh and grabbed the package.

"I got some snacks and juice boxes, too. Wasn't sure what you'd want the kids to have, but..."

She took the other bag he handed her and looked inside it, avoiding his gaze. He'd thought of buying food for the twins? She set the bag on the floor and reached around Savannah to open the diaper package.

"This is for you." His peculiar tone drew her gaze. He held another plastic bag toward her, this one bulging with something soft.

"What is it?"

He just pushed it farther toward her, glancing away as if he were...embarrassed?

She took the bag, almost afraid to see what it held. Clothes? She pulled out the green item on top.

A hooded sweatshirt, *Green Bay Packers* emblazoned on the front with the football team's logo.

"There are sweatpants in there, too." He scratched the back of his neck with his fingers.

Heat surged through her, warming her before she could even put on the sweatshirt. She set the clothing beside her leg on the seat, not able to lift her gaze.

"Sorry, they're men's sizes. But at least they'll keep you warmer."

"Thanks." She managed to push out the word, hating the warmth that crawled into her face, probably turning her cheeks red. Good grief. It wasn't like no guy had ever done anything nice for her before. Not exactly.

She lifted Savannah and set her in the car seat again, then pulled the sweatshirt over her head. Savannah started to cry, and Sammy asked his favorite *What that* question, giving Valena an excuse to stay busy and ignore the gaze she could feel Cooper had locked on her.

As she began the messy task of changing diapers, the soft sweatshirt wrapped her in a cocoon of warmth that couldn't rival the heat emanating from her racing heart within. Maybe she'd wait on calling the police. Just a little while longer.

▭

Cooper kept his eyes glued to the snowy, ice-covered road while his mind traversed ground just as slippery. He had to get that phone away from Valena somehow.

The screen had been bright when Cooper had gotten in the

car at the gas station. She'd been using it for something. Hopefully just random Internet surfing.

But he knew she was smarter than that. She had probably been trying to figure out where they were. Maybe trying to contact someone.

His stomach cinched.

If she'd called or texted anyone, their location could already be compromised. Bad enough that guy had shown up at the car. Cooper still felt uneasy about him, especially since he'd driven off after Cooper had shooed him away instead of going into the convenience store to get directions. Good he drove off. Bad if he reported something to the wrong people.

Cooper glanced in the rearview mirror to check on his passengers.

Savannah slept now, apparently happy to be cleaned up with a fresh diaper. Sammy, on the other hand, was just revving up after snoozing through the overnight adventures. This three-minute pause was the longest silence they'd had since leaving the gas station, as Sammy peppered Valena with constant questions. Or rather, one question repeated over and over again.

At least he was keeping Valena too busy to use her phone.

Please, Lord, show me how to get her to turn off her phone, peacefully. Another prayer. Valena was having a strange effect on him.

More likely it'd simply been a long time since he'd had this much at stake. Lance, his friend and a man who trusted him with his most precious loved ones, was in trouble. He was counting on Cooper to keep his kids safe until he could make it back home.

Cooper would not let him down, no matter how cute or stubborn the kids' nanny was.

He carefully slowed on the slippery road, an odd surface of snow crusted with a layer of ice on top. The cottage driveway should be there somewhere, but the gray sky cast flat lighting everywhere, eliminating any shadows to distinguish white-shrouded driveway from snow-buried ditch. Hopefully, it would have been too hard for anyone else to find it, too.

"What that?" Sammy's favorite question drew Cooper's attention to a spot of black amid the snow.

"It's a mailbox." Valena never seemed to tire of answering the boy with the infinite patience Cooper remembered his mother having with his younger sister.

The mailbox marked the end of the driveway he was looking for. He'd almost missed it, thanks to its sideways tilt under a layer of snow. Must have met the business end of a snowplow, though there wasn't much evidence of one coming through recently. At least the ice on top of the snow meant their car wouldn't get stuck in the driveway.

"Why?"

Cooper grinned at Sammy's favorite follow-up question as he slowly turned into the tree-lined driveway. Most of the boy's interrogations seemed to center around the snow. "Has he ever seen snow before?" Cooper glanced in the mirror.

"No." Valena's tone was softer than it had been before they'd stopped for diapers, but she seemed to be avoiding his gaze. Did she feel guilty because she had called someone on her phone?

He hoped there was some other explanation. Maybe she was truly getting worried about being in this remote location with him. The letter should fix that.

But if she had used her phone…there could be more than a letter from Lance waiting for them at the cottage.

"What's that?" A higher-pitched voice seemed like a delayed echo of Sammy's.

Cooper laughed, the natural response bursting through his rising tension as he glanced in the mirror to see Savannah straining to look out her window. "Didn't know she was awake."

"Just." Valena glanced away from the mirror as soon as he swung his gaze her way, but he caught the surprise in her violet eyes.

Why surprise, he didn't know. It was going to take a while to figure out this puzzle that was Valena Greer.

He pulled the car around the wooded curve of the long driveway.

The two-story cottage stood in a cleared area amid the trees, backed up close to the lake behind it. No welcome committee had formed yet, at least that he could see.

His tight shoulders loosened a fraction. There was plenty of opportunity for concealment in the woods that surrounded the cottage on both sides. He'd have to be on his guard.

"That's a cottage?"

He grinned, Valena's sarcastic question easing his tension even more as he pulled the car in front of the structure that was more like a mansion by most people's standards. "From Lance and Miriam's point of view."

"If he really works for the DEA, how could they afford something like this?"

Always thinking. She might have left the science field behind, but she certainly hadn't turned off her brain. "It was technically Miriam's. She inherited it. From her grandparents, I think. She could certainly afford to keep it. She was a doctor, you know."

"Oh, so that part is true?" The defiant edge to her tone was back in full force, along with the spark in her eyes that made him want to stare.

He pulled his gaze away from her reflection in the mirror and turned off the car. "I'm not picking and choosing the truth here." He rotated in the seat so he could see her without the mirror. "I'm sorry things are this way, but it's not my fault Lance's work required him to be less than open with you."

"Less than open?" Those breathtaking eyes widened. "Wow, that's typical. You think you can call lying whatever you want and do whatever you want so long as it's 'for our safety.'" She made air quotes with her fingers around the last words. "Do you know how many times I've heard that copout?"

Oops. Clearly stepped on a hidden mine there.

"Eat me?"

Cooper couldn't hold back the laugh that sprang from his lips at Sammy's question.

"He means he's hungry." Valena glared at Cooper, but he thought he caught a slight twitch at the corner of her mouth, as if she was fighting a smile.

"I'm hungry, too, buddy." He smiled at Sammy, whose blue-eyed gaze drifted his way. "We'll get you something to eat when we get inside, okay?"

"Eat me?" Sammy repeated the question.

Cooper chuckled. "Let's get them inside before the cold hits the car." He looked at Valena, who hadn't made a move to get the kids out yet. He tried a smile. "You'll love the inside. It's really souped-up. Lance put a lot of work into it."

"I've never liked Lance's obsession with technology and inventions, if that's what you mean." But she started to undo Savannah's car seat buckle anyway.

Cooper tried to hold back a grin as he got out and scanned the silent winter wonderland. Still clear, and the lady was cooperating. So far, so good.

He opened the back door by Sammy and spotted Valena's bare feet beneath the green sweatpants she'd rolled up at the ankles. Realization slammed into him. Had she walked barefoot at the air strip when they'd switched from the plane to the car? It was freezing.

What was wrong with him? He'd been so focused on making sure they weren't spotted or tailed when they transferred that he hadn't paid attention. He only noticed she'd refused to use a blanket for herself. His irritation at that might have made him less aware of her needs, too.

Guilt wadded in his throat. "Hang on a sec." He bent down and took off his tennis shoes, socked feet landing on the ice-crusted snow. He reached across Sammy in the car seat and handed her the shoes.

She stared at them, but didn't move.

Stubborn woman. "Look, this ground is cold, and the kids are going to freeze. Can we hurry?"

It worked.

She grabbed the shoes from his hands. They'd be huge on her, but hopefully she could tie the laces tight enough to keep them on for the short walk to the door. At least she didn't protest this time when he lifted Sammy out of the car seat.

"How about I take Savannah, too? So you can manage with those shoes?"

She gave him a glare.

He lifted his free hand in surrender. "Fine."

"What ear?" Sammy's little fingers touched the edge of Cooper's ear, gently for the most part.

"Yeah, that's my ear. You have ears, too, don't you?" Cooper talked with Sammy as he walked a short distance from the car while Valena got out on the other side. He checked the surroundings again.

The crisp air was pin-drop still. Except for a shuffling sound.

He turned back to see Valena scootching her feet along the ice while holding Savannah, wrapped in blankets. He nearly had to bite his tongue to hold back the laugh that wanted to escape.

The sight of Valena, drowning in the oversized sweats and

sliding one foot at a time in shoes that could be a clown getup on her, had to be the most adorable thing he'd ever seen. And the most beautiful.

His heart lurched in a way it had no business doing.

His grin vanished. He had a job to do. He didn't need attraction for a woman clouding his focus. And he didn't need the pain that came in the end. Been there, done that. The image of Gillian when she'd said her sudden goodbye blocked his vision of Valena.

He was not going to let history repeat itself. He would keep his distance and do his job, happily parting ways when it was all over.

He marched toward Valena. "Here, let me take her. You're going to take an hour to get in the house at this rate."

A flash of surprise flickered in her eyes. Maybe hurt, too.

He swallowed the guilt that slipped a sour taste into his mouth as he reached for Savannah. He was nearly as surprised as Valena when she let him take the girl.

He turned away and carried the kids to the cottage, eyes and ears peeled for any visitors. He needed to stay focused on his job, not the cute nanny.

The place seemed secure, for the moment.

It wouldn't last.

CHAPTER
NINE

SHE SHOULD HAVE JUST WALKED on her bare feet to the door, never mind she already felt like a Popsicle playing dress-up in Cooper's oversized shoes. She'd forgotten just how cold Wisconsin was.

Valena reached the large entry door where Cooper waited with the blanket-wrapped twins, both of them burying their little hands in his hair.

Must mean the short locks were as soft and thick as they looked.

She pushed aside the ridiculous thought. She was about to enter an unknown house in the wilderness with a total stranger. Who had a gun. "I can take them now." She reached for Savannah, but the girl leaned harder against Cooper.

Valena had to keep her mouth from dropping open. Savannah always wanted to come to her. Cooper was a stranger.

"They're fine." He managed to reach his hand out from under Sammy to press his thumb against a small black screen attached to the wall. What was a fingerprint reader doing at a cottage in the middle of nowhere?

A click sounded, and Cooper opened the door, entering first with the twins.

Valena stepped inside behind him, hit by the warmth of the shelter and the sheer size of the place. She shouldn't be surprised after living in Lance's and Miriam's Florida mansion for two years.

"Welcome."

She jumped at the female voice and scanned the great room for its source.

"Please identify yourself." Sounded like a computer.

Lance. Trying to shake the unnerving feeling she'd just stepped into a sci-fi movie, she stifled a sigh as Cooper answered with his name.

How long had it taken Lance to rig that? She'd hoped fighting him to keep his computerized home idea out of the Florida house would make him stop wasting time on artificial things. He could've spent that valuable time with his children.

"Voice pattern verified. There's someone with you." The female voice was starting to grate on Valena's nerves.

Cooper looked at her.

She rolled her eyes. "Valena Greer."

"Voice pattern verified. Welcome."

Exactly what would've happen if they hadn't been verified anyway? Maybe she didn't want to know.

"Are the children with you?"

Valena started at the electronic woman's question. This had to be a joke. Like she was going to have a conversation with a computer.

She'd nearly had to threaten Lance with quitting to stop him from computerizing the Florida house. They both knew she would never leave the twins, but at least her protest had shown how seriously she did not want their home to be so artificial. They already had a nanny for a mom and a nearly imaginary dad. That was artificial enough for any child.

"Yes." Apparently Cooper didn't mind chatting with computers. "Samuel and Savannah are here."

"Good."

Valena rolled her eyes again at the computer's response. She stepped out of Cooper's oversized shoes, her cold feet landing on the hardwood. She looked up at Cooper to grill him about when Lance had spent so much time fooling around at the cottage. But the words faded on her lips at the sight he made with a child on each arm.

Savannah leaned her head against his neck while Sammy traced lines on his face, following the chiseled features with a little finger. Her babies were tiny in his arms. Protected.

He looked strangely at ease holding them. Strangely…right.

Her chest squeezed with an emotion she wasn't about to define.

Bored with his face game, Sammy started to squirm.

Valena sucked in a much-needed breath. "I'll take them now." She stepped closer, arms extended.

Thank goodness Sammy leaned toward her instantly.

She started to take him into her arms.

"Hold it." Cooper's warning made her pause and tense, ready to defend her claim on the children.

"Hang on." He chuckled, a deep velvety sound close to her ear. Far too close.

Her pulse picked up speed as her breathing grew shallow.

"His blanket's twisted around my hand."

That explained the tug and the warm skin that brushed her hand as Cooper freed the blanket. Didn't explain the zing that shot from the tips of her fingers to her bare toes when he leaned close to tuck the loose end of the blanket between her and Sammy.

His gaze flitted up and crashed into hers. His brown eyes darkened.

Her mouth dried to sandpaper.

His gaze lowered.

To her lips?

A well-timed body kick from Sammy shattered the moment, sending her back a step as she steadied him in her arms.

"You want to hold her, too?" Cooper's eyes and expression were back to neutral, as if nothing odd had happened.

Good. Maybe it hadn't been anything. Her mouth had been dry already. She hadn't drunk anything for hours.

"Just set her down." Valena wasn't about to risk another transfer, certainly not before her heart rate returned to a normal healthy range.

"I don't want her wandering, though. I need to clear the rest of the house. You and the kids need to stay by the door."

Valena grabbed Savannah's hand as her ping-ponging emotions landed on irritation. He had to stop giving orders. She shouldn't have even followed him this far with the twins. And now he was trying to unnerve her. Exactly like he'd done with that harmless tourist at the gas station.

She'd show him she wasn't falling for it. "Who could possibly be waiting for us? We just flew across the country."

He looked at her with a steady gaze, no irritation sparking in his eyes. "You'd be surprised. I'd feel better if you'd agreed to leave your phone behind."

The phone again. "And the twins and I would feel better if you'd left us at home."

There was the glint of frustration she was waiting for. "Believe me, nothing could be further from the truth."

The gravity of his tone sent a shiver up her spine. An image flared in her mind—the big men at the house, running over the roof with guns. Too late, she tried to hide her reaction so he wouldn't know his line had the effect he'd wanted.

But he had turned around, anyway, headed across the great

room. Typical male. Why bother to communicate when you can just walk away?

He gripped the doorknob of a closed door tucked in one wall.

"The toy closet is now unlocked."

Valena jumped at the computerized female voice. Blast Lance and his stupid tech obsession. She took a breath, hoping her racing pulse would get a chance to calm down sometime soon.

Cooper swung the door open and let out a low whistle that sent her overactive heart on another sprint.

Nerves. She seriously needed to chill.

"Looks like the kids won't get bored." Cooper threw her a smile she steeled herself against. "Tons of cool toys in there."

She raised an eyebrow. "I'll be the judge of that." She pulled her gaze away from him before her heart gave out from sheer exhaustion. She feigned a deep interest in the cottage, scanning the first floor, which she could see most of thanks to an open floor plan.

Cooper opened more doors along the walls, looking for imaginary boogie men while she got her bearings.

A large sitting area with oversized sofas took up the center of the space, a flat-panel TV hanging above a fireplace. The kitchen that opened to the great room had a middle island and a bar counter with stools. A large dining table stood on the near side of the bar.

Why Lance and Miriam would need a place equipped to entertain ten people, she couldn't fathom. Not out here in northern Wisconsin wilderness.

Unless this wasn't their place at all. She resisted the urge to bite her lip, hiding the concern that thought inspired as Cooper walked past her toward the stairs near the front door.

How did she really know this was Lance's place? She was

just taking Cooper's word for it. But even with the extreme computerization, it didn't have to belong to Lance.

She watched Cooper until he disappeared on the top floor. She dropped Savannah's hand and lowered Sammy to the floor.

"Eat me?"

She touched Sammy's head. "In a little bit, sweetie."

"My blankie soft…" Savannah unwrapped the blanket from her shoulders as she started telling one of her stories, which Valena couldn't listen to at the moment.

Grabbing her phone from the sweatpants' pocket, she checked for messages. None. No answer from Lance.

And her battery was at a quarter now.

She'd have to make a decision before it dropped to zero. To call the police or not.

Sammy and Savannah wandered over to the toy closet, and Valena followed, trying to make her choice.

Cooper had left her alone now. He might not again. Especially if—

The phone vibrated in her hand, giving her a jolt of surprise.

A phone call. ID listed an unknown number. Should she answer? She wouldn't normally unless she knew the caller. But this situation was far from normal. Maybe Lance was using a different number to reach her.

She pressed the icon to answer the call. "Hello?"

"Hello, Valena." A man's voice.

She froze.

"I'm Special Agent Hinds. I'm with the DEA." His tone was calm, in control.

Not another one. Her breath returned at the familiar sound of a government type trying to play her. This, she could handle.

"I know you've taken Lance Acker's children."

"Excuse me?" Irritation shot through her torso, sending needed heat into her arms. "I didn't kidnap them, if that's what you're insinuating. I'm their legal guardian."

"Is Cooper White with you right now?"

Her stomach tightened. It was one thing to know the twins weren't at home and assume they were with the nanny. But how did he know Cooper was with her? She shouldn't be surprised. The government always knew more than it should.

She turned away from the toy closet where the children played and looked up at the balcony above.

No sign of Cooper.

"No."

"Good."

She turned back to Sammy and Savannah as they worked together to pull a large, rideable truck out from the bottom shelf, Savannah chatting about its red and green colors.

"Don't trust White. He's not who you think. He's probably told you that you need to run and hide the children. Am I right?"

Her breath caught. Had she been right about Cooper? Her suspicions that he wasn't the good guy grew in her mind. But she wouldn't give this man the satisfaction if he was trying to play her. "Get to the point, Mr. Hinds."

"Agent Hinds. White is lying to you, Valena."

The sound of her name on his tongue scraped across her nerves.

"The DEA is fully capable of taking care of the children during this time when their father is...busy." His momentary pause echoed more loudly than his words in Valena's ear.

"So exactly why should I believe you over Cooper? I know even less about you than I do about him. You could be a terrorist, for all I—"

"Valena Jane Greer, graduated from the University of Florida with two degrees, a Bachelor of Science in Physics and a Bachelor of Science in Biochemistry. Oldest of three children —younger brother Roger Carlton, Jr., twenty, and younger sister Brittany Joy, nineteen. You don't see your siblings much, since they live in California. Your father, Colonel Roger Greer, serves in the Army. His postings during your childhood took you to all but six U.S. states and to Djibouti. Your father got you the position as nanny for the children of Lance Acker, an Army acquaintance of your father's."

Lance knew her dad? She didn't know that. Neither of them ever told her. How dare they? She thought the recommendation had come through her mom's friend, not her father.

"I can list all the states you've lived in, if you like, and the years. And then, of course, there's the date of your parent's divorce and—"

"That's enough. I believe you're government." Only people in government had so much information and weren't afraid to use it to get what they wanted. "What's going on? Where is Lance, and who were the two men who broke into his house in Florida?"

"I can't share that information with you."

Of course.

"You only need to know that we at the DEA are the people you can trust. We're the only ones who can keep Acker's children safe while he's away. It's what Lance would've wanted."

Would have? Could Lance be dead? She moistened her lips. "If you're the one who can keep the children safe, why didn't you rescue them back at the house? Why did Cooper have to do that?"

A pause. Maybe didn't have that covered in his notes. "I regret to have to tell you this, but White's intent may not be to rescue the children at all. We're not sure what his plans are for them."

She'd had the same suspicions herself but for some reason

they sounded worse, harder to believe, coming from someone else. Especially a government agent. "Are you saying he's dangerous?"

"We're not at all comfortable with White's actions."

"He says he used to be one of you—DEA. Is that true?"

A longer beat. Was he checking to see if he could tell her that? Frustration tightened her muscles. Government bureaucracy and their need-to-know nonsense.

"White was associated with the DEA at one time."

A careful answer. "Was he an agent?"

"I can't say anything else right now. But I need your help, Valena. We need you to help get the children safely away from White. Can you do that?"

"But he's one of you."

"We're not at all certain where his loyalties lie. I don't believe the children are safe with him." His words piled onto the growing mound of doubts in her mind.

"What are you doing?" Cooper's angry voice sounded right behind her.

CHAPTER
TEN

VALENA JERKED THE PHONE DOWN, her thumb pressing the screen to end the clandestine call as she spun toward him. Her delicate nostrils flared, and her smooth cheeks were tinged with pink.

Cooper's thoughts stalled. Hadn't meant to end up so close to her, close enough to fall into those violet eyes. Close enough to forget his anger in the power of the current that sizzled between them. Almost.

"I told you not to use your phone." His voice came out gruffer than he intended, thanks to the sudden thickness in his throat. "Don't you realize what could happen to them?" He took advantage of the moment to step out of electricity range and look at the kids, who pushed toy train cars out of the closet past Valena. Of course, she'd ignored his instruction to stay put with the kids at the front door.

"How dare you?" Her eyes flashed. "I care more about the safety of the twins than anyone else does."

"More than Lance?"

"Given his behavior over the last year, probably so." Her slim jaw tightened. "And if anything you've told me is true, then he knowingly put them in danger through his work or whatever he's actually doing."

"That isn't fair. Lance cares about keeping his kids safe. He put me in place to ensure they're protected." He took a step toward her, meeting her challenging stare. "Somebody has to do the hard jobs."

"Oh, please." She crossed her arms over the baggy sweatshirt. "*Somebody* doesn't have to be a dad with a little girl who needs him more than the government."

Cooper tilted his head, her wording and the pain underlying her tone not lost on him. She clearly wasn't talking about the kids anymore. His heart softened.

Her cheeks flushed red, the anger in her eyes not able to mask all the hurt. "Or a little boy like Sammy." Her attempt to cover the slip came too late.

He took another step toward her, risking the electric danger zone around her. "Valena, maybe your dad—"

"What do you know about my dad? About me?" She stepped away, then turned back. "Who are you anyway?"

"I told you."

"You told me the safe, photoshopped story that you expect me to swallow without any questions. There's more to you and what you want with me and the twins than you're telling me." She planted her hands on her hips, emphasizing how tiny she was underneath the billowy clothing. "You said you'd show me proof that Lance knows you and hired you to protect the twins, but I have yet to see it. And I want more than a nice story about Lance and Miriam."

"I said you'd have proof, and I meant it. I just thought you might want to get the kids in warmer clothes first." He pulled the folded paper out of his back pocket. "Here it is." He held out the letter.

She took it and unfolded the paper.

"Recognize the handwriting?"

Her gaze lifted briefly, more irritation than affirmation in her eyes.

He watched as she silently read the letter. Her lush eyelashes hovered just above her smooth skin, and her rose-colored lips pursed slightly as she read.

He dragged his gaze away, hoping to stop the out-of-bounds direction of his thoughts. She didn't even like him, let alone what he did for a living. That should be enough reason to avoid adding more relationship baggage to the load he was already lugging around.

He watched the kids play with more toys from the closet. The kids he'd sworn to protect. He shouldn't be getting distracted. He should be thinking of an escape plan.

He'd heard enough of Valena's phone conversation to guess who was on the other end. Maybe Jack. Could be Baker or Cross. Or worse, Hinds.

All that mattered was she'd been talking to a DEA agent. Which meant the cottage was no longer safe. They must have called Valena—on the phone she'd refused to turn off or leave behind. He'd have to do something about that now, whether she liked it or not.

"Okay." Her tired voice reached for him, and he turned toward her, an odd twinge tightening his chest at the defeat that marked her brow. "I guess you win."

The *I-told-you-so* he'd planned to say after she read the letter washed away with the wave of something much softer that settled in his core. He reached to touch her shoulder, but dropped his hand short and angled away, toward the children. "The kids win."

Valena drew in a breath and faced the children, as well.

The little ones played on the floor without a care in the world, without any idea that they'd become targets of one of the most dangerous organizations he'd faced. Then again, Valena didn't know that yet either.

He sneaked a glance at her out the corner of his eyes.

Her defiant stance, crossed arms and fixed jaw, had already returned.

He did not want to be the one to break the bad news.

━━

"You've got to be kidding me." Showered and in warm women's clothing that Lance had apparently stocked at the cottage for such an occasion, Valena stood refreshed and ready to handle Cooper. She took a wide stance in her new boots and leveled him with a hard stare.

He looked irritatingly unintimidated, slouching back on the sofa with one long leg propped at the ankle on his knee and his toned arms stretched out from his sides to rest on the back cushions. "No. We—"

"Absolutely not." She walked to Savannah and scooped her up from the floor, sweeping up the plastic cube she was playing with along with her. "You just uprooted us from the only home the twins have ever known." They'd only been at the cottage for less than two hours, and he already wanted to move them again?

A tingle of nerves made her aware of the risk she'd taken in leaving Cooper alone with the twins while she had showered. What if he'd decided to take them wherever he wanted, without her? She'd rushed through her shower and putting on the turtleneck, sweater, and jeans. Probably was only gone fifteen minutes versus the hour it had taken to bathe the twins and get them into the winter clothes Lance had stockpiled at the cottage. Apparently some time during that period, wanderlust had claimed Cooper again. Already. She had sure pegged him.

She wasn't going to let a roots-phobic man bring insecurity into her babies' lives. She met Cooper's gaze, ignoring the charge that shot to her toes even across the twenty feet that separated her from where he sat. "I won't let you upset the twins any further."

"This red." Savannah pressed a red button on the cube that started cheerful music and lights, totally incompatible with the tense conversation going on around her.

"They don't act upset."

Of all the nerve. "Excuse me?"

He shrugged. "I'm just saying I think you're overly worried. Kids are resilient."

"Oh, and you have how many children?"

His jaw shifted. No ready answer.

"I didn't think so. What you have no clue about is that children need routine and stability in their lives. That's where they get their security. Without security, they'll—"

"Be in danger?" He got to his feet and sauntered the distance between them with the confidence of someone who knew he'd won an argument.

What an exasperating…The thought trailed away with the breath in her lungs as he moved into her space and stopped closer than she'd expected.

The black sweater he'd donned complimented his tanned skin tone and darkened his eyes to a distracting chocolate color. "You read Lance's letter. You know I'm here for a reason, and you need to trust me." He leaned his head toward her, robbing her of her last bit of air. "The kids are in serious danger. Valena…" a shiver crawled up her arms under the sweater as he breathed her name, "trust me."

She couldn't look away. She wanted to trust h—

"We have to leave now." The added command swung a jolt of reality like a sledge hammer into the spell he'd somehow cast over her.

She stepped back. He was good. Really good at whatever

game he was playing. She would've thought she'd be a much tougher mark.

But Lance's letter said he was for real.

Cooper is my closest friend. The only man I'd trust with my life and my children. He'll protect them to the best of his ability.

She took in some much needed air and turned away, adjusting her hold on Savannah.

"See?" Savannah pressed another button on the cube, starting up a different song.

"Yes, I see." Valena murmured the words as Savannah tried to sing along. Even if Lance did trust Cooper, that didn't mean the man would be a protector or friend to her. She had to be the one to make the call for the twins' health and well-being. Lance's letter had confirmed that, too. But what if Cooper was right about the danger? Lance's letter only talked about Cooper and the children. It said no specifics about this situation, other than admitting he was a DEA agent.

She faced Cooper again. "I need to know what's going on. If you want me to uproot the twins again, I need a reason."

He opened his mouth—

"More than you telling me they're in danger. I need the facts." Great. She sounded like her dad. Shoving the unhelpful observation aside, she held Cooper's gaze.

He ran a hand over his hair, leaving one clump sticking up at his crown.

How was it that he suddenly looked like an endearing little boy? She fought to keep her expression hard.

"Okay." He looked at his wristwatch. "But we have to make this quick. They could be here in thirty minutes. Assuming I was right on their start location."

"Who could be here?"

He looked at her as if still determining how much she needed to know.

She braced her jaw and lowered Savannah to the floor

before she gave in to the urge to start yelling at Cooper over the girl's head. She straightened and managed to calmly face him. "I know about the DEA."

Not even a flicker of surprise touched his eyes. He must have heard more of the phone call than she'd thought.

"You'd better start talking, or I'll have no choice but to believe what the agent told me."

"Oh, you mean the agent you talked to on the phone you weren't supposed to use?"

She glared at him. "Seriously? You're challenging *me* right now?"

"We don't have time for this. Believe me, the less you know, the better."

She let out a humorless laugh. "That is so typical."

"What?" His eyes snapped.

"Keeping secrets might make you feel more in control, but it doesn't protect anybody but you. So, no. I don't believe you." Just another selfish male, keeping his distance and control by putting up a wall of secrets.

"Security alert." The computer woman's voice made Valena start. "Unknown vehicle approaching. Estimated arrival time, six minutes."

"That's it. We need to go." Cooper spurred into action, moving for Sammy where he played on the floor.

"Don't touch him."

He grabbed Sammy anyway.

Fury shot through Valena's veins as she stalked over to him. "I said—"

"I get that you don't trust me." Answering fire flamed in his gaze. "But Lance did." He turned and headed for the opening to the back hallway. "I'm not going to let these kids get hurt."

She scooped up Savannah and followed him. Whatever he was

doing now, she wasn't going to leave him alone with Sammy. She hurried to catch up to his long, quick strides. "Do you even know who's coming? It can't possibly be the same men from Florida."

He stopped at the back door where two toddler-sized snowsuits hung alongside two adult jackets. "Hopefully not." He grabbed both suits off the rack on the wall and handed one to Valena. "Put this on Savannah. Hurry."

Valena took the suit but hesitated, watching him crouch down to put the other one on Sammy. "Are we running from the DEA?"

"Sort of."

"Sort of?" The man was insane. "I'm not running from a government agency unless you have a really good reason."

He paused and stared up at her, piercing her with intense brown eyes. "They'll take the kids from you. How's that for a reason?"

"But…they can't. I'm their legal guardian."

"The DEA has a hundred ways they could manage it, at least until they get what they want." He zipped up Sammy's suit and stood, turning to face her. "There's more going on than you know. You'll just have to trust me." He reached to take the suit from her.

She pulled it back. "I'll do it."

"Hurry." He grabbed the black jacket off the rack and slipped it on.

She squatted in front of Savannah, a smile lighting the girl's face as she saw she was going to play dress-up again. "We need diapers, food—"

"I packed what I could into those."

She turned her head to catch his gesture toward two backpacks that leaned against the wall by the back door. He must've packed them while she had bathed the kids.

"Aren't we taking the car?" She held Savannah up with an

arm around her as the girl slid her foot through the leg of the suit.

"Can't." He hurriedly helped Sammy into pull-on boots that looked slightly large for him. "There's only one road in and out."

"Then what are we going to do?" She zipped up the suit and took the other pair of boots he handed her, helping Savannah slip her feet into them.

He silently picked up one backpack and held out the blue jacket from the rack.

"Why do I have the feeling I'm not going to like your plan?"

He met her gaze, sending a jolt of awareness through her. "I have the feeling you're going to hate it."

She took the jacket and shoved her arms into the sleeves as he lifted Sammy and went out the back door. Valena looked at Savannah, playing with the zipper of her new snowsuit. Should they really run from the DEA? With a stranger?

"They'll take the kids from you."

An alarm blared through the house.

"Unauthorized entry attempted." The computerized woman sounded as calm as before, but Valena's pulse jumped into action.

She grabbed the backpack and slid her arm through one strap. Hefting Savannah, she jogged through the door without looking back.

CHAPTER
ELEVEN

THE BLAST of the security alarm escaped through the back door of the cottage.

Cooper straightened from putting Sammy into the snowmobile trailer.

Valena burst out, running with Savannah in her arms.

Thank you, Lord.

Valena put on the brakes, staring at his getaway solution. "What is that?"

"You've never seen a snowmobile?"

"Of course I have. That's your plan for outrunning them? What's that thing on the back?"

"It's a trailer for kids."

She shook her head, the stubborn expression he was coming to know well sliding into place. "I'm not letting the twins ride in that. It's too dangerous."

"You can ride with them the whole time."

"You can't outrun a car with a snowmobile anyway."

"Won't have to. We're going that way." He pointed at the lake and moved toward her to take Savannah.

She pulled the girl closer, angling away, a horrified expression widening her mouth as she stared at the frozen body of water. "On the ice?"

"Valena, do you hear that alarm?" His adrenaline-charged muscles twitched to yank Savannah from her arms, but he battled the urge. "They're here. They'll be around back in ten seconds if we're lucky. They *will* take the kids from you, and everything Lance worked for will be destroyed."

She loosened her hold on Savannah.

Cooper grabbed her. "Get in. I'll hand her to you."

For once, Valena did what he said and quickly entered the enclosed trailer, sitting next to Sammy.

He passed her Savannah, and she sat the girl on her lap.

Valena's gaze collided with his as he pulled back. Actual fear lit her eyes, something he hadn't seen before despite all they'd been through. "Be careful."

He nodded. "I promise." He closed the door of the trailer and hopped onto the snowmobile.

It coughed as it started, making enough noise to alert every DEA agent in the state.

Please, Father, let this idea work.

He took off, slowly at first, checking behind to be sure the trailer stayed attached. Everything looked good.

Except for the guy in the black jacket jogging around the corner of the cottage.

Cooper sped up, heading straight for the lake sixty feet ahead. He glanced back.

The agent had his weapon out, but Cooper banked on him not shooting. It would risk the kids at this distance. He hoped the agent knew that.

Cooper looked over his shoulder in time to see two more men join the first.

Hinds. Cooper would know that red hair anywhere. Hinds might shoot Cooper just for the fun of it.

But he was almost to the lake.

The men gained on him.

He looked ahead, zoomed the snowmobile down the slope of the beach and onto snow-covered ice.

He prayed the ice was solid, despite the fluctuating temps lately.

Hitting the flat surface, he opened up the speed. He glanced back to see the distance he was putting between himself and the men.

They were trying to run on the ice after him but making slow progress.

He looked ahead of the snowmobile for a few seconds before checking behind again.

Looked like they might not be moving now as they quickly became featureless stalks on the horizon. He let out a breath as he faced forward again.

A noise reached his ears amid the cold wind blasting his face. Crying?

He twisted to look at the trailer.

It bounced and jerked thanks to bumps on the ice.

He slowed a little, glancing farther back to be sure the agents had given up.

Couldn't see them anymore.

Now he just had to pray Valena didn't do something crazy like pop out of the moving trailer before they reached land on the other side. And that the DEA didn't manage to reach the opposite shore faster than he'd estimated. Cutting across the lake instead of having to drive around should make a difference of twenty minutes. He sent up a prayer that would be enough time.

A vibration moved against his abs. His phone in the jacket pocket. He wouldn't take his focus off of driving his precious cargo long enough to check, but it should be a message from Jenkin, hopefully saying he was in place.

Thank you, Lord.

He looked at the trailer, where the crying seemed to have stopped.

Something dark caught his gaze a long distance behind.

He looked forward to check where he was going, then immediately glanced back again.

An SUV?

His muscles tensed.

Hinds. He'd never risk losing twenty minutes on them. Even if he didn't know the ice was solid enough to hold an SUV.

Cooper accelerated the snowmobile, praying Jenkin was in place and ready to get away fast. If he wasn't, they were in serious trouble.

━━

Valena gritted her teeth against the bouncing as she squeezed the twins close, trying to absorb as much of the jostling as she could.

Savannah's crying had made her right ear go numb, but Sammy giggled and squealed.

When Cooper had sped up again, she'd looked out the small rear window and spotted the SUV trailing them.

She couldn't see much ahead. They'd better be close to land, or they wouldn't have a chance of outrunning the SUV. If that's what she should hope at all.

What if Cooper was wrong about the DEA? Why in the world would they be after Lance's children or want to take them from her, the guardian Lance had chosen?

Maybe he didn't really work for them as Cooper had claimed and Lance confessed in his letter. What if Lance was some sort of criminal instead?

That would explain the DEA's serious interest in him and why they would chase her and the twins across a frozen lake.

She reminded herself to breathe. If only she knew the truth. Who to trust. Lance told her to trust Cooper in the letter, but Lance had lied to her for years. She didn't even know if she should trust him anymore.

The snowmobile slowed and tipped up, as if they were climbing a hill. They must have reached the shore.

She loosened her grip on the kids enough to turn to see out the back.

The SUV was halfway across the lake.

The snowmobile stopped.

Cooper jogged to the trailer and yanked the door open. "Hurry, they're almost here." He grabbed Savannah as he talked and shifted her to one arm. "I'll take him, too."

She handed him Sammy and got out of the cramped trailer. "How are we going to—" Her gaze landed on a navy blue jeep, parked at the edge of the tree line on top of the short hill.

"Follow me." Cooper trudged quickly up the snow-covered slope.

She jogged to catch up. She shouldn't have let him carry both twins. He was getting too far ahead with them. But she didn't hear any crying. Even Savannah had stopped. Weird.

She froze as a big man walked around the jeep toward Cooper and the twins. He stood even taller than Cooper with a build like Thor from the movies.

"Man, am I glad to see you." Cooper's tone was friendly as he continued forward. The guy must be okay.

The big man hurried toward Valena. "Hey, there." He flashed a broad grin, long blond hair curling out from under his blue beanie. "Need any help? The snow's slippery here."

She caught his glance behind her to check on their pursuer, though he didn't lose his friendly smile. She pushed faster up the slick hill. "No, thanks."

"Okay." Another grin. The guy was downright cheerful, which seemed totally out of place given the circumstances.

She reached the jeep as Cooper put Savannah in a seat next to Sammy. "There are no car seats."

"Would you just get in?" Tension stretched Cooper's voice as he stepped aside and swung an arm toward the vehicle. "They're almost here, and Jenkin's the best driver I know."

Jenkin must be the Thor dude sliding into the front seat.

She hesitated. Another strange car with two strange men this time.

A soft touch on her arm brought her gaze back to Cooper. "I won't let anything happen to them."

She shivered. From the cold, of course, not his touch. "You better not." She stepped into the jeep and lifted Savannah to settle on the seat, holding the girl on her lap and tucking Sammy against her side.

Doubt attacked her mind. What choice did she have? Lance's letter had said to trust Cooper. Didn't that mean she should?

The jeep took off too fast, and she gripped the armrest of the door beside her.

Her heart thumped in her ears. Who was she kidding? She'd spent her whole childhood trusting the wrong man. A man very much like Cooper.

She slid her hand to the door handle. Could she somehow make a dash for it? Maybe if Cooper's pal slowed or stopped?

"Valena." Cooper's voice froze the panicked rush of her thoughts.

She jerked her gaze to see those dark eyes trained on her from the front seat.

But there was no warning or threat in his eyes. Only compassion...and promise?

"Trust me."

Could she? She searched his gaze.

He didn't look away.

But she did. She let her hand slip off the door handle. She would trust him for this moment, with protecting the twins in this jeep. But anything beyond that, she couldn't give him.

She would never put her trust in the wrong man again.

CHAPTER TWELVE

"NICE JOB, MAN." Cooper checked the passenger side mirror from the front seat. Still no sign of the DEA agents since they'd left the woods. "Haven't lost your driving skills. Even if you do live in Mayberry."

Jenkin chuckled as he watched the curving road. "Hey, I'll have you know I work out of the third-largest city in Wisconsin."

"Impressive." Cooper laughed at his friend's feigned pride. Good thing for him Jenkin had chosen to stay in Wisconsin after completing the protection job that introduced him to the woman who was now his wife. Cooper couldn't have pulled off this quick getaway without his old pal.

"I'm thinking it's a pretty good thing you set up this Security League." Jenkin sent him a grin as he echoed Cooper's thoughts.

"One of my few good ideas, I guess." Cooper chuckled. He might've been able to call Jenkin anyway, given that they were personal friends. But the Security League's secure communication app meant he already knew where Jenkin and other private security specialists were located, and he could instantly communicate needs he had with any of them as needed.

The app was another good thing Lance had helped Cooper with, providing the technology to ensure the Security League's communications and data were secure even from government monitoring. Perfect for occasions like this one.

"Can we stop somewhere for the kids?" Valena's tone from the back seat was anything but amused. "They're not happy, and we need car seats."

Sammy said something unintelligible in a whiny voice, as if to prove her point.

Cooper shared a glance with Jenkin. Of course they couldn't stop. Jenkin had done a great job losing the DEA, but they would easily get back on the trail if Cooper made a mistake like that.

The kids just needed something to do. The package.

"I almost forgot." He reached into the backpack on the floor at his feet. "There's a present for them."

"A present?"

"From Lance. I found it at the cottage." Cooper pulled out the flat package, gift-wrapped in yellow paper with a red stick-on bow, and handed it to Valena.

She looked at the tag he'd already read at the cottage. "To Samuel and Savannah, for every birthday and Christmas I will miss. Forgive me. I love you. Daddy." She glanced at Cooper, her eyes glittering as if moist. But she tensed her jaw. "They'd rather have him here."

A lump clogged Cooper's throat. Had Valena caught the farewell tone in Lance's note? He hoped it wasn't confirmation of what he feared might happen.

Valena tore open the wrapping paper. "It's an iPad." Disappointment weighted her tone.

A yellow post-it was attached to the screen.

"What does the note say?"

Valena looked down. "V, hope twins enjoy the games."

"Cool." Cooper smiled, trying to put a positive spin on the situation. "I've heard of kids their age using games on iPads."

Valena frowned. "Not my kids. It's unhealthy."

"I thought there were some educational games or something."

"Go down." Savannah squirmed as if she was trying to slide out of Valena's arms, her features scrunched with a squealing whine.

"Look, this will keep them entertained for a little while longer." Cooper met Valena's gaze over Savannah's head. "We don't have far to go."

Valena sighed and turned on the device.

Cooper rotated to face forward in his seat and caught his friend's grin. "What?"

"You two sure generate a lot of sparks."

Cooper glanced back to see if Valena had heard the quiet comment, but she was busy helping Sammy hold the iPad. He looked at Jenkin, tempted to set him straight. But he'd better not risk Valena overhearing any response. "How's Tamara?"

Jenkin slanted him a twinkling glance that signaled he was wise to the subject change. "You can ask her yourself. She's meeting us with my cousin's van."

"You're kidding."

Jenkin shook his head. "She'll never stay home out of harm's way. Likes to keep me worried, I guess." A smile stretched his face.

"And you love it."

There was no missing the bliss on Jenkin's face. "Nine months of marriage, and I'm wondering how I ever lived without her."

"Happy for you, man." Cooper tried to ignore the envy that clustered like a heavy block settling in his stomach. What would that be like? To have a perfect partner, supporter, friend.

"C is for Cooper."

Cooper jerked at the sound of his name in a computerized voice from the iPad.

Valena's startled gaze met his own.

He laughed. "Lance must have designed that game, or at least tweaked it. He always said he wanted to do game design. I didn't know he'd gotten around to it. That's cool he did that for his kids."

The computerized voice continued to call out more normal words with letters as Sammy and Savannah touched the screen.

"He should have spent that time with his children." Valena watched Cooper instead of the game.

"Maybe he wanted to give them something they could enjoy for a long time."

"Like a father?" The bitterness in her tone suggested they'd again gone beyond Lance to something much deeper for her.

He knew how to deal with the DEA and their other pursuers, but the shadows of her past? He hoped they didn't prove to be the most dangerous enemy.

━━

What little sunlight there had been was fading away, leaving the gray skies to transition to charcoal, one step away from the black darkness of night.

Valena fought a shiver as she settled Sammy onto the bench seat of the old van they were switching to. A van without car seats.

"I'm sorry we can't go the rest of the way with you."

Valena glanced out the open door to see Tamara balancing

Savannah naturally on one hip. Jenkin's wife grabbed her full lip with her teeth, doing nothing to detract from the beautiful picture she made with her long wavy hair cascading from beneath her crocheted hat.

Women so naturally stunning usually made Valena feel insecure at best, especially when she was dressed in clothes that weren't a perfect fit and wore a man's winter jacket. But something about Tamara's peaceful, nurturing demeanor made Valena almost wish she could stick around, too.

Maybe if they weren't out in the deep woods on some hermit's driveway or remote gravel road to nowhere.

"I could help with the kids."

Valena stepped out of the van and took Savannah. "We're used to going it alone."

"You do it well."

Valena went back into the van, hearing Tamara step closer behind her.

"But sometimes the best kind of help is the help we didn't know we needed."

Valena looked up from setting Savannah on the seat next to Sammy.

A slight smile curved Tamara's lips, her eyes holding an expression that backed up the impression she meant more by that statement than help with the twins. Tamara turned her head to look at the men who shook hands by Jenkin's jeep, saying something Valena couldn't make out.

Tamara angled back to Valena. "I haven't known Cooper long, but Jenkin speaks highly of him."

Valena dropped out of the van beside Tamara. Her gaze found its way to Cooper.

"Jenkin says he's a good man. And those are hard to find, aren't they?" Tamara looked at Valena. The understanding in her brown eyes bridged the stranger gap between them, as if

Tamara could see through the walls of hurt forged by the years around Valena's heart.

She glanced away, to Valena's relief.

"You ladies done chatting yet?" Jenkin grinned as he and Cooper approached the van.

Tamara answered with a warm smile. "We were just waiting for you men to get done with your visit."

Cooper let out a snort while Jenkin laughed. Jenkin gently tugged Tamara to his side, and they smiled at each other in mutual adoration.

Valena felt Cooper's gaze on her, but she glanced at the kids in the back seat, Sammy playing with the smart pad he couldn't get enough of. "We need car seats."

Cooper's frown signaled he'd heard her mutter. "When we're somewhere safe."

"I hope we've lost the tail for good." Jenkin watched them with a somber expression instead of his usual grin. "But be careful."

Cooper nodded and headed around the van to the driver's side.

Valena turned to enter the back with the twins.

"Valena." Tamara's voice held her back.

Valena turned to see Tamara standing behind her.

"Take care of yourself and those precious twins." Tamara enveloped Valena in a hug.

Valena blinked, but then returned the embrace, moisture pricking her eyes as warmth filled her chest.

When Tamara pulled back, her gaze glistened, too. "And don't be afraid to let him take care of you all." She glanced at Cooper, then back to Valena.

"Thank you."

Valena climbed into the van, lifting Savannah onto her lap and keeping Sammy close.

Cooper took off, Valena watching Jenkin and Tamara in the fading dusk until they were gone.

"Cool people, aren't they?" Cooper watched her in the rearview mirror.

Had he heard what Tamara had said about him? Defenses raised, Valena looked away from his gaze. "I was just wondering why they're your friends."

"Ouch. The lady jokes."

She glanced at the mirror in time to see his eyes crinkle with a grin.

Her pulse fluttered. Ignoring the rebel inside, she kept her expression firm. "We need car seats."

His smile dropped. "Valena, we're in the middle of nowhere, and we need to stay there until we figure out—"

"It's illegal to have children ride without car seats."

He was silent for a moment. Had she actually gotten him? "We're running from the DEA."

Nope. And he had a point. "It's still unsafe."

"I care about the kids' safety, too."

She raised her eyebrows. "Prove it."

"Where are we going to find a place to buy car seats out here?"

"I'll find somewhere." She reached in the jacket pocket for her phone. The pocket was empty. And she had no memory of putting the phone there. Or in her jeans' pockets.

Oh, no. Had she lost it in one of the vehicles? In the snowmobile trailer?

She thought back to when she had seen it last. At the cottage. Before her shower. She had left it on the bed in the room. When she came out of the bathroom in the new clothes, did she forget to look for it?

She remembered looking at the room, curious if it had belonged to Miriam and Lance or if it was a guest room. She couldn't recall seeing her phone on the bed. She would've grabbed it if it had been there.

An explanation formed in her mind, and she narrowed her eyes at the headrest behind Cooper. "Where's my phone?"

His silence and the way he avoided her gaze in the mirror provided her answer.

"You took it?"

"The battery was dead." Which he could only have known if he'd looked at it.

And Tamara thought Valena should trust this guy? "How dare you take my phone." Fury strangled her voice. "You had no right to do that."

"You were jeopardizing the kids' safety by using it." His eyes flashed in the mirror. "How do you think the DEA found us so quickly?"

"That's it. Stop the van."

"Valena—"

"Right now. I'm not riding another minute with a thief and a liar."

"I did what was necessary to keep the kids safe."

"*I* get to decide what's best for them. Remember Lance's letter?"

"That letter also told you to trust me."

She glared at his reflection. "Then give me a reason to. You still haven't told me what's going on. Or was your promise to tell me just another lie?"

"I haven't lied to you." Steel lined his voice. "The less you know, the safer you'll be."

Not that line again.

"But since you don't believe that either, I'll tell you what I know."

Her stomach clenched. What if she didn't like what she heard?

"Those thugs you mistook for burglars are from a Columbian drug cartel."

Good thing Cooper was driving so he couldn't see the surprise that probably showed on her face. She knew Florida had a problem with drug-runners. But in Lance's house?

"Lance has been working on a case involving the cartel for a long time. They have a presence in Florida, but they've spread elsewhere in the U.S."

"So that's what he was doing in Columbia?"

"He's working with Columbian officials and went undercover with the cartel. Trying to find its root."

"Why?"

"To cut off its head."

"Just how much danger is he in?"

Cooper met her gaze in the mirror, eyes darkening. "It's a ruthless cartel."

A tremor passed through her, leaving her colder. "They're after the children?"

She looked at Sammy beside her, the iPad abandoned in his lap as he gave in to sleep. Savannah rested the back of her head against Valena's neck, also quiet and sleepy.

Her angels. And their lives were in jeopardy.

"Wh—" The word choked on the emotion jamming her throat. She cleared it and tried again. "Why do they want the twins?"

"I'm not sure." Cooper's gaze was softer as he looked at her, then back to the snow-covered road ahead. "Last I heard from Lance, he said he was on to something. A way to cripple the cartel. He said it wasn't where he thought. We got cut off before he could tell me more." He took in a deep breath. "I'm guessing whatever he was on to scared the cartel. That's why they're after the kids."

"But the twins wouldn't know anything."

"If they have the kids, they'll have a hold over Lance. A way to lure him to them or kill whatever his plan is."

Horror rose in her chest, threatening to cut off her air supply. Her babies, wanted for bait by a violent drug cartel? Images of what could happen to them if they were caught raced in front of her eyes. She pressed a hand over her mouth to hold back the surge of vomit that seeped up her throat.

"Whoa." Cooper slowed the van and pulled to the side of the narrow road.

He was suddenly squatting in front of her, apparently having climbed over the console to reach the back seat. "Valena." He gently spoke her name until she met his gaze, her stomach still churning.

"I won't let anything happen to the twins." His brown eyes looked deeply into hers. "Trust me."

"Trust you?" She transferred her horror to the stare she pinned on him. "Their own father got them into this. He chose to put them in harm's way. What makes you think for one second I would trust his pal to keep them safe when men like you are the reason they're in danger in the first place?"

Savannah murmured and lifted her head.

Valena tried to calm her breathing, find a neutral expression and heart rate that wouldn't scare Savannah. She and Sammy didn't need fighting and conflict to add to their trauma.

"Men like us." Cooper's voice was deep, level and controlled, resonating as he stood, stooped above her because of the low ceiling. "Men like us are the ones who do the dirty work. The work no one else wants to do, no one talks about. Lance wanted to make the world, our country, a safer place for his kids to grow up."

He turned away, but his final statement drifted back. "And he may have to give his life for it."

His life? "Wait."

Cooper paused by the front seat.

"Lance could die?"

Cooper looked back, his gaze meeting hers. "The cartel has his number. They play for keeps."

DREAD STIRRED Valena's stomach as she stared at the small structure at the end of the driveway. Its silhouette stood like a snow-capped black cage that even the surrounding army of trees couldn't penetrate.

"Where are we?" She kept her voice soft, not wanting to wake Savannah, who slumped in her arms, or Sammy, asleep on the seat beside her.

"The cabin belongs to Jenkin's cousin. Or her family. Same people who own this van we're driving."

He pulled the van to a halt facing the cabin.

Little moonlight could find them through the thickly clustered trees. Or maybe it never shone there.

She forced a swallow. "We can't stay here."

"You're not going to be a snob, are you? I know it's nothing compared to Lance's cottage, but I'm sure it's livable."

That was like saying the White House was slightly more glamourous than their Army base housing in Texas. "It doesn't look safe...for the twins." She couldn't tear her gaze from the pitch blackness of the interior she could see through small windows. "Does it have electricity?"

"It better. I'll go check it out." Cooper scrounged around in the glove compartment and pulled out a heavy-duty flashlight. "Jenkin to the rescue." He tossed her a grin probably meant to put her at ease.

It didn't.

He dropped out of the van, leaving the flashlight off as he walked to the cabin.

She didn't miss the way he scanned his surroundings in the dark. Why hadn't he left the headlights on so he could see?

"Makes you a target."

She mentally shoved the voice of her dad away. He hadn't been in her head for a long time. Why was he bothering her now?

Cooper. That was why.

She watched as he pressed his back to the wall by the door, then swung in front of it with his gun and flashlight pointed inside.

Her breath caught.

Just like her dad. Always making her feel tense and unsafe, vulnerable and alone in the scary world he said was so dangerous for her. All the while seeking out the danger like an addict seeks a fix. How ironic a carbon copy of her dad was the only protection in sight for her babies now.

If she believed in God, she'd say He must be having a good laugh about that one. But God was even less real than her dad.

A clear beam split the darkness of the square windows as Cooper moved through the tiny cabin with the flashlight.

Then he appeared again, coming out safely.

She let out the breath she hadn't realized she'd been holding.

But why was the cabin still dark?

Cooper approached the van and opened the driver's door.

He looked into the back seat as he sat down. He smiled at the twins. A smile that made her stomach flip.

"Still sleeping?" He kept his voice quiet. Almost a whisper.

She nodded, careful not to move Savannah. "What about the lights?"

"The power seems to be out. Probably the ice storm that came through. Found a generator, though. I can hook it up and get it running."

Her heart pounded, but she battled to keep the growing fear from her voice. "The twins will be too cold."

"It's actually not very cold inside, and there's a fireplace. I'll build a fire first, and you can keep the kids by it while I start the generator."

"Can't we keep driving instead?"

"I think we'll all feel better if we get a little sleep. No one should be able to find us here. Not tonight."

"I can sleep in the van while you drive." She hoped he didn't detect the stress in her voice.

"You haven't slept at all." He looked at her with a gentleness in his gaze that made her elevated pulse thud in her ears.

"I will. Or I can drive so you can get some rest."

The corner of his lips tugged into a smile. "I'll sleep when I know you're all safe and warm inside."

He exited the van before she could stop him with another excuse. The side door opened, and he stepped up next to the bench seat. He looked at her over the twins. "Think they'll stay asleep?"

Why did his whisper send a shiver through her? Probably the cold air he was letting in. "Maybe. They're way more tired than usual." *Thanks to him*, she reminded herself.

Holding on to irritation kept the fear at bay as she carried Savannah to the cabin, following Cooper and Sammy.

Until a crack punctuated the night.

She jerked toward the sound.

Dark woods greeted her searching gaze, their blackness growing thick just past the eerily shadowed perimeter that bordered the cabin.

"Mhmm." Savannah shifted her head against Valena's shoulder.

Valena hurried to catch Cooper, trailing him to the doorway of the cabin.

She froze.

Darkness engulfed the interior.

A beam of light swung her way. Cooper's flashlight.

"Want me to take her?" His arms were empty.

"What did you do with Sammy?" Fear torqued her stomach.

"Relax. I laid him on the sofa." He flicked the flashlight to illumine Sammy's small form, slumbering on the green sofa. "Are you okay?" He swung the beam in her direction.

"Fine." She snapped out the word with more force than she intended.

Cooper walked the few steps between them and handed her the flashlight. "I'll get a fire started."

She aimed the flashlight at Sammy again as she clutched Savannah close, heart knocking against her ribs. She tried to deepen her breathing, keep it together.

She stared at the beam of the flashlight in her hand. There was light. She was in control. There was still light.

Something clanged, making her jump.

Cooper picked up the poker he must have dropped in front of the fireplace.

The sound shouldn't scare her. It meant she wasn't alone. She focused on her breathing, counting the seconds as she stared at the flashlight beam.

An eternity later, the strike of a match announced the arrival of a tiny flame. Then a small orange glow started at the base of the wood Cooper had stacked in the fireplace. The flame crawled over the logs to grow bigger, creating an aura of light in the fireplace.

Valena drew toward it, standing within the boundaries of the soft illumination. If only it would chase more of the shadows from the room.

But she could make out a narrow bookcase on one wall and the outline of a table with four folding chairs not far from the sofa. Anything beyond that was hidden in darkness.

"I'll work on getting the generator started and grab the backpacks from the van. I'll need the flashlight so I can see what I'm doing."

Her heart smashed into her ribcage. She couldn't let him take the light.

He paused in front of her, tilting his head to meet her gaze. "Are you sure you're okay?" Those intense eyes searched hers.

She couldn't let him see weakness. Her dad would remind her that's what it was. Weakness. She needed to be strong. She should laugh at danger like her dad always did. "Of course. I'm fine." She thrust the flashlight into his hand.

His mouth pressed into a line. "Fine." He disappeared with the flashlight before she was ready to face the darkness alone.

But it wasn't dark. She had a fire. And she didn't need Cooper. She was being ridiculous.

Would she never learn? He wasn't some hero she could depend on. He was the guy who'd essentially kidnapped her and the twins, stolen her phone, and was probably lying to her about the reasons why.

He still refused to tell her anything true about the DEA. Nothing about why Agent Hinds had called her or why the DEA was chasing them. What if Hinds had told her the truth? Could Cooper be on the side of the cartel?

It would be smart of him to tell her about the cartel wanting to kidnap the twins. The information made him appear innocent and trustworthy.

But Lance's letter. He'd said to trust Cooper.

What if Lance himself had been fooled? That could be why he was in danger now. Because he'd trusted Cooper. The man she and the twins were alone with in the wilderness.

The flame flickered, as if a gust from somewhere was trying to snuff it out.

Had someone opened the door?

"Cooper?" She whispered his name, scanning the darkness that surrounded the edges of the fire's glow. Why had she let him take the flashlight?

The glow decreased.

She jerked to check the fire.

It was dying.

"No." Her heart pounded, blood rushing like a thundering waterfall in her ears.

She set Savannah on the sofa and hurried to the fireplace, dropping to her knees in front of it. She bent over and blew on the flame, trying to make it bigger. Her panicked breath came out too hard.

The flame went out. Only red embers remained.

"No." The word broke as panic choked her. Darkness surrounded her. She scrambled to her feet. Had to get to the twins. But she couldn't see.

A creak.

Her heart stopped. She peered through the darkness for the source of the sound near the far wall.

A hand reached through the open window.

CHAPTER
FOURTEEN

A SCREAM SHATTERED THE STILLNESS, shooting straight to Cooper's heart.

Valena.

He whipped out his weapon as he sprinted from the back of the cabin to the front. He forced himself to pause against the wall by the door.

No sound from inside.

He slammed open the door and swung into the room, flashlight and weapon leveled.

Violet eyes blinked.

"Valena? What—"

She stepped into him, slipping her arms around his torso. Her body trembled against him, her breathing shaky. "I thought I saw something."

He holstered his gun and returned the embrace with one hand while he held the flashlight in the other. "What was it?"

"Nothing. I looked again, and it was nothing." Her voice caught on the last word, as if a sob choked it.

His heart squeezed so hard he thought it would burst. "I'm here now. It's okay." But it wasn't okay. He'd never heard anything like her scream. Nothing that had seared through his soul with such pain. The thought that she might be hurt or—

"Leave your weapon in—"

Cooper had it out and Valena shoved behind him before the man could finish his sentence.

A tall man stood in the doorway, illuminated and hopefully blinded by Cooper's flashlight. But the guy didn't lower his gun.

"Who are you?"

"I could ask you folks the same question." The man curled a grin that was far from friendly. "I know the folks that own this cabin. You ain't them. Now I suggest you lower your weapon before you're looking at a felony charge."

Brown pants, tan shirt, dark leather jacket. And a sheriff's badge that bounced back the beam Cooper shone on it. The guy was law enforcement?

"Identify yourself." Cooper kept his gun trained.

"Deputy Brian Hanson. Lower your weapon before the lady and those twins get hurt."

How did he know about the twins? The darkness covered them on the sofa. Unless…

Realization pushed more adrenaline through Cooper's veins. But Hanson had his gun already out and aimed. Too risky to make a move until he relaxed.

Cooper lowered his weapon and angled the flashlight away from the deputy's face.

"That's it. Now put the weapon on the floor real slow and easy, and you and the lady back away. You're all going to have to take a ride with me."

"Okay." Cooper slowly bent over as if he was going to comply, then threw the flashlight at the deputy's hand.

The gun went off as Cooper lunged at Hanson, taking down the deputy. He grabbed the tactical flashlight from the floor and landed a glancing blow with the handle. The deputy's head slumped back against the floor.

"Why did you do that?"

Crying, probably from Savannah, pierced the cabin as Cooper pressed his fingers against Hanson's neck.

His pulse was strong.

"He's fine. Just out." Cooper got to his feet, grabbed the deputy's Glock, and tucked it in his waistband behind his back. He picked up the flashlight and his own weapon, holstering it.

"But why did you do that?" The size of Valena's eyes matched the incredulity in her tone. "Do you realize we could get—"

"Arrested? No." He went to Savannah, and she stretched out her little arms to be picked up. "He's a dirty cop." Stepping back to Valena, he handed her the crying girl.

"What?" Confusion fogged the violet of her eyes as she automatically took Savannah.

"He couldn't have known about the twins unless someone told him." Cooper went back to the sofa and lifted Sammy, who was somehow still sleeping. "And he came in silent. Must've left his car farther away and walked in."

"Isn't that normal procedure when he suspects someone broke into a home?"

Cooper carried Sammy outside, forcing her to follow. "Not unless he had warning in advance somebody could be here. And that we were armed. He had to know."

"Know what?" The question sounded out of breath as she hurried to keep up with his quick pace.

He stopped at the van and freed one arm to slide open the back door. "Who we are and that we could be here."

"Cooper." He stopped short at the unfamiliar sound of his name on her lips. He met her gaze.

Confusion and apprehension swirled in her eyes. "You just

left a cop unconscious in there. I need to know why. If you want me to trust you, you need to trust me."

She was right. He nodded. "Get in, and I'll tell you everything."

She got in the back with the children, holding one in each arm, their bodies leaning against her as he slid onto the driver's seat and pulled the extra Glock from behind his back.

He stashed it in the glove compartment and started the van.

No sign of the deputy as he turned the van around and drove away.

"I'm ready."

Figured she wouldn't waste any time. He glanced at her in the mirror, briefly meeting her level gaze in the shadows as she stroked Savannah's hair, calming the girl's cries to soft whimpers. "The DEA has a leak. That's why Lance is in the spot he's in."

Cooper swung the van onto the gravel road. "He had to stop reporting in with the information and evidence he was gathering on the cartel when he learned they had a source in the DEA. But it might have been too late. The cartel had gotten wind of a snitch in their own ranks and were becoming suspicious of everyone."

"And they figured out Lance was the mole?" Concern weighted her question.

"The DEA snitch must have found out and told them."

The headlights of the van caught the outline of a vehicle.

The deputy's car, parked alongside the narrow road.

Cooper slowed as he drove past, scanning the vehicle to make sure no one waited inside. It was dark. Empty.

"Won't the deputy call more police? Report that we assaulted him?"

"No." Cooper sped up, rounding a curve in the road. "He

won't want his department to know he's working for the cartel."

"What? In Wisconsin?"

"The drug business is everywhere."

"But I thought the DEA must have sent him."

"The DEA sends agents, not sheriff's deputies. I'm sure the snitch in the DEA got word to the cartel by now that we're in this area. Probably alerted their contacts to search remote locations. That's why he wanted to take us for a ride."

She didn't respond or make a sound for several moments.

He checked on her through the mirror.

She was watching him. "Is Lance still alive?"

Cooper's throat tightened. "As long as the cartel is going after his kids, they haven't killed him yet. If they stop wanting the kids for leverage…"

"But they can't get the twins. And we can't keep running like this." Valena's voice thickened with emotion. "What can we do?"

We. Warmth traveled through his chest. "I've been trying to contact Lance at the remote voicemail we have set up for emergencies. I check it often. He said he would contact me there if something like this happened."

"What if he doesn't?" The hopelessness of her tone twisted his gut.

"Then we'll figure something out. If I can find out what evidence Lance had and what the big thing was that he mentioned, I could finish it for him. I could nail the cartel before they get to the twins."

"Why hasn't Lance contacted us? It's like he cares even less than I thought."

Cooper looked in the mirror to grab her gaze. "He loves his kids. You can be sure he's doing everything in his power to help them and stay alive, if he can. The fact that he hasn't left me a message is..." He gripped the steering wheel. "He's having to be extremely careful, or he could be injured."

He glanced at her again, then back at the road. "You should probably prepare for the worst."

The sunrise battled with darkness, slowly winning as the sky turned a lighter shade of gray. Valena sat in the front passenger seat and watched the landscape of endless flat fields covered with snow as they drove on a two-lane highway.

She angled to look back at the twins, sleeping in the car seats Cooper had finally let them stop to buy. How could she prepare two-year-olds for the death of their only remaining parent? The question rolled her stomach, already queasy from the deficit of sleep and food. "Where are you taking us now?"

Cooper turned his head toward her. The growing light revealed a shadow of stubble that outlined his firm jaw and did annoying things to her heartbeat. "You should get some sleep while you can."

Gorgeous or not, the man was exasperating with his evasiveness. "I can't sleep when I don't even know where we're going." She folded her arms over her sweater, chilled from the draft that seemed to seep through the doors of the van. She glanced back to check on the twins. Both slept soundly in the car seats she'd bought at the first department store they had come across. "The twins need structure and stability to feel secure."

"They do, or you do?" He reached to turn up the heater, but anger was already starting a fire in her belly.

She opened her mouth to respond.

"I'm sorry."

She shut her mouth. That was the last thing she'd expected him to say.

"I just meant they're happy and safe right now. But what I said was uncalled for." He twisted his hands on the steering wheel and let out a sigh. "Lance told me about your dad."

She turned away, stiffening.

"His record is amazing. A real dedicated soldier."

She stared out the windshield, letting a sardonic smile angle her mouth. "Yeah. He's dedicated all right."

Silence fell between them.

"But not as a father."

She jerked her gaze to Cooper.

He met her surprise briefly with a compassionate gaze. "I know the demands of military service. A record like your dad's doesn't come without sacrifices."

She swallowed back the lump building in her throat. "Some things should never be sacrificed."

"No. They shouldn't." Understanding deepened his voice.

Moisture pricked her eyes. She blinked it back. She would not let it get to her. Not in front of Cooper. She cleared her throat. "Did you know Lance served under him?"

"Under your dad? Yes."

"I didn't even know they knew each other until I read Lance's letter." Though Agent Hinds had told her minutes before the letter confirmed it. "I should've figured he'd still be controlling my life if he could."

"Sounds like your dad at least cares about you."

She leveled a glare at Cooper. "There's a big difference between caring and controlling. We're like toy soldiers to my dad. Strategically positioned where he wants us and then left to our own..." A realization lit her mind. "Wait a minute."

"What?"

She dug in the backpack on the floor by her feet. Her fingers found the paper. "Got it."

"Lance's letter?" Cooper cast her a glance, his dark eyebrows lifted. "What about it?"

She unfolded the letter. "What if Lance is trying to position us? Tell us where we need to go?" She scanned the handwritten contents. Her gaze locked on the phrase she was looking for. "Listen to this: 'I'm so glad I bumped into your dad that day in Chicago, and he told me you were looking for a job.'"

"Yeah?" Lines crossed Cooper's brow.

"My dad has never been to Chicago. Illinois is one of the states we never lived in."

"So Lance…"

"…knew I would know that. I think he's giving us a clue."

"Way to go, Valena." Cooper sent her a grin that made her pulse skip a beat. "Chicago, here we come. I have a friend who can probably put us up at his apartment."

Another one? "Just how many friends do you have across the Midwest?"

His brown eyes twinkled. "Enough so I never have to pay to stay anywhere when I travel through."

"We do have the ten thousand dollars Lance left for you at the cottage." Another secret Cooper had kept until he deemed she 'needed to know' to buy the car seats.

"Minus the car seats expense, but yeah." His full lips pressed out slightly as he watched the road. "We'll be easier to find if we stay at a hotel. We might have to risk it eventually, but if we have a safer option, we need to take it."

Always making the decisions no matter what she thought. She pressed her teeth together. "Pretty sure of yourself, aren't you?"

His brows pulled together as he glanced her way. "This is what I do."

"What if you make the wrong call someday?"

"I pray that doesn't happen and hope God will help me make it right if it does."

She stared at him. "You pray?"

"Yes. Does that surprise you?"

She shrugged. "Just wouldn't have pegged you as the type."

He winced. "Why is that?"

"You're the independent, action-junkie type of guy. You have what it takes to get the job done, and anything that doesn't go according to plan is just more fun."

He didn't look at her, but she saw the movement of a swallow along his neck.

"Men like you don't want anything to lean on. Or anyone." And she would do well to keep that in mind before her heart got ideas about this particular man.

"I'll do my best to keep us safe, Valena. But in a situation like the one we're in," he looked at her, his eyes dark and grim, "I suggest you start praying, too."

FIFTEEN

Chicago, Illinois

COOPER BURST through the door to the apartment. "I've got it." He halted, shocked by the sight before him. His friend Bobby fit the bachelor stereotype to a tee, and his apartment had been a pigsty of spoiled pizza, empty bottles, and soiled laundry when Cooper had left to pick up groceries.

Now the apartment practically sparkled.

"What have you got?"

Cooper's gaze found Valena standing by the counter behind the twins, both seated on the full-backed bar stools.

"Hi." Savannah smiled as she greeted him.

Sammy followed suit by lifting his little hand to wave.

Cooper's chest squeezed. How he'd love to be greeted like that every day. "Hi, guys." He walked over and set the grocery bag on the gleaming counter, glancing at Valena. "How in the world did you get this place cleaned up so fast?"

She shrugged. "Elbow grease and organization. My mom could clean every new place we moved to in two hours, no matter how bad it was. A surface clean, anyway." She pulled the grocery bag toward her. "So you got the stuff."

"Yes, but that's not what I meant. Can I see the letter again?"

Her smooth brow furrowed as she pulled Lance's letter from her back pocket. "Sure."

"When you read it to me in the car, I didn't pick up on anything odd because I thought any other clues would be meant for you to figure out. But getting out in the city brought it all back."

"Brought what back?" She turned those violet eyes on him, and he nearly lost his train of thought.

The letter. He laid it on the counter and scanned for the part he needed to confirm. "That's it." He tapped the line of Lance's handwriting. "He meant for me to get this one."

Valena stepped closer to read the sentence, close enough to up his heart rate. "Ask Cooper about the time he saved my life. Then you'll know why I trust him." She looked up at him.

Her violet eyes at that proximity sent a jolt through his system. "When did you save his life?"

He had the vague sense she'd asked him something, but he couldn't pull himself out of those eyes.

"Eat me?" Sammy's question brought Cooper to attention.

Savannah giggled. "Eat, eat, eat, eat!"

Cooper laughed and reached into the grocery bag. He pulled out the pre-packaged snack packs of crackers, cheese, and juice Valena had instructed him to get for this emergency. Veggies and other healthier items were also in the bag for Valena to cook later. If they were still at the apartment then.

"Cheese!" Sammy shouted, a wide smile brightening his face.

"Cheesy, cheesy, cheesy!" Savannah chanted in a singsong as she bounced on the stool.

Valena reached to steady her, meeting Cooper's grin with a smile.

His heart nearly stopped.

He'd never seen her smile up close. At him. The beauty of it robbed him of air.

"So about the clue." She opened the lunch packages and set them in front of each child as if she had no idea she'd just found a crack in his armor.

"Right." He swallowed, his mouth suddenly dry. "It happened here in Chicago. I didn't exactly save his life, but we were working a case together and things got dangerous. I backed him up when he needed it."

"And that's a clue somehow?"

"I think it must be, since he brought us here." Cooper shrugged off his jacket and walked to the sofa to toss the jacket over the back. "We had a hiding spot for that case that no one else but our informant knew about. It was how we communicated with him." Cooper returned and leaned his hands on the countertop. "I heard that guy died in prison six months ago. The spot would be safe to use, if Lance needed to hide something."

She helped Sammy stack a rectangular piece of ham onto a cracker. "What do you think he hid there?"

"I don't know. But I'm sure it will help us get closer to ending this."

Savannah struggled to push the straw into the juice pouch, and Cooper moved behind her to insert it for her.

"Do you think that's what the clues are for?" A whisper of hope fringed Valena's question.

"I'm sure of it. Lance always has a fail-safe for everything. He knew the cartel would come after the kids. I know he prepared for this part of it, too. As much as he could."

"You really think he's going to...that they'll..." She glanced at the children, but they happily munched on their food.

"The cartel knew where to find his kids, which means his

cover is completely blown. That information is extremely protected. But the mole in the DEA still somehow got it. That's not a good sign."

"How can I tell them?" Her voice choked, and she looked away, smoothing her fingers over Sammy's silky hair.

A lump blocked Cooper's throat. "Whatever happens, Lance is counting on us to keep the twins safe."

She nodded, her lips forming a firm line. "We will."

Another *we*. Warmth spread through his torso.

"So when do we go to the hiding spot?"

"It's not a part of the city I'd want you and the kids going to."

Her mouth flipped into a frown. "Oh."

"And it's too risky to go during the day anyway. I think we lost our tails for the moment, but I don't want to chance leading them to whatever Lance left for us. I'll wait until dark and then go alone."

Her gaze flitted across his before she looked down to brush crumbs off the counter into her hand. Was that apprehension in her eyes?

He stepped around Savannah to reach into the grocery bag again, finding the cell phone box. "I got you this." He pulled it out of the bag.

Her eyebrows shot up as she looked from the box to his face.

"It's a burner phone we can ditch tomorrow and get a new one. I'll program it with my cell number so you can call me or text if you need anything." He reached into his pocket, feeling the tiny plastic square there. "I don't like to leave you, but you'll be safe here tonight. And I'll leave you the deputy's gun. Do you know how to use a gun?"

"My father's a colonel." Her gaze emphasized the apparent ignorance of his question.

"Right." Confession time. He pulled out the memory card from her old phone and held it up between his finger and thumb. "I'm sorry for taking your phone."

Her eyes glistened as she lifted her gaze from the memory card to his face. Were those tears?

His stomach twisted.

She glanced away. "I have photos of the twins on there. I never wanted them online or anything because I thought that would make the children vulnerable." She looked at him, the moisture gone. "I guess that seems pretty stupid now." Her lips trembled, sending a shot of pain to his heart.

He stepped closer, but stopped himself from taking her in his arms. "Not stupid at all. You were trying to protect them. You've always done that and done it well. That's why Lance trusted you so much."

She tilted her head slightly as she met Cooper's gaze. "I admit, you've done a pretty good job of that yourself the last two days."

His heart pulsed against his ribcage under her appraisal.

"I'm…sorry I didn't believe you at first."

"No problem. I like a smart woman." The words were out before he thought. But he didn't regret them when she widened her eyes, and the hint of a smile caressed her lips.

He couldn't stop a grin. "Though a little less stubborn might be nice."

The full smile curved her mouth. "Don't count on it."

He laughed and handed her the memory card.

A current shot through him as their fingers touched.

Those violet eyes searched his face. Had she felt it, too?

His gaze dropped to her lips.

"Do you ever sleep?"

He blinked. Not exactly what he was thinking about at the moment. "Only when it's safe."

"Then you'll sleep now."

"I don't—"

"You just said we were safe here."

"For the moment."

"Then for the moment, you need to sleep." She met his gaze with an unblinking stare. "You just noted how stubborn I am." She plunked her hands on her hips. "Do you really think you're going to win this one?"

Amusement and annoyance battled in his mind. How could one tiny woman produce such conflicting emotions? Not to mention the desire to kiss that stubborn set of lips.

Whoa, Cooper. Maybe she was right. He was past the point of being able to control his mind, which meant he'd better rest. "Okay, you win."

The smile she beamed was a prize worth any compromise.

"But I'll only sleep for thirty minutes."

"Ninety."

"Sixty."

"Seventy-five."

His lips twitched as he held back a grin. "You'll need to keep the door locked and check out the window every fifteen minutes. Actually, make it ten. If you approach with your back to the wall and just barely pull the blinds away from the window, you can see without being seen. And wake me at any sign of d—"

"That's enough. You need a nap." She quickly got behind him and pushed him toward the hallway that led to the bedroom.

Heat traveled across his back at the touch of her small hands through his sweater.

He turned around and grinned at her. Bad idea. The urge to kiss her multiplied by a hundred.

"Ena, what that?"

"Go to bed." Valena softened the command with a smile as she spun away to attend to Sammy.

Cooper headed for the bedroom, trying to keep his mind on the adventure awaiting him tonight. But the little lady in the next room was proving to be the most exciting adventure he'd ever experienced.

———

Valena's eyes popped open. Where was she? The room was unfamiliar. A martial arts poster hung on the wall above a television opposite where she sat on a ratty sofa.

The apartment of Cooper's friend. Everything came rushing back.

Cooper was gone to find whatever Lance had left for them. She was alone with the twins. She'd intended to keep watch in the living room. Must have fallen asleep.

She walked to the bedroom, flicking on the hall light as she went.

The twins lay asleep in the bed, snuggled under the sheet and thin blanket she'd found, hopefully clean, in the hall closet.

Strange how quiet this apartment building and neighborhood were. She'd lived in enough cities to know that quiet at night wasn't normal.

A sense of foreboding skipped her pulse at the thought.

It was deadly quiet.

She walked back to the living room, her gaze finding the door to the apartment.

Looked like it was still locked.

She went to double-check. She tried to turn the knob. It didn't budge.

It was locked. Good. But she'd forgotten to turn the bolt as Cooper had commanded when he left.

She turned it now.

The click rang out as loud as a laugh at a funeral.

She willed her heart rate to calm. There was no reason to freak out.

A creak sounded outside the door.

CHAPTER
SIXTEEN

FOOTSTEPS ECHOED, drifting up toward Cooper. He moved back from the railing of the fire escape and waited.

A man passed underneath, glimpses of his silver jacket breaking through the holes of the metal platform beneath Cooper's feet.

The guy—looked like a teenager from his slight build—paused midway into the alley. In this neighborhood at two a.m., the kid was probably in trouble or about to cause some.

A flame sparked as the kid lit a joint. Great. Better not be planning to hide in the alley the whole time he smoked it.

He turned and left the way he had come.

Cooper let out a breath and swung back to the brick wall of the old apartment building. He touched the brick above the farthest corner of the landing he stood on and counted three up, six out.

He leaned into the railing on the corner, stretching to reach the loosened brick, if it was still there. He gripped the edge with his fingers and pulled.

The brick came loose.

Thank you, Lord.

He set the brick on the platform by his feet to ensure

he didn't drop it, then felt inside the pocket in the wall. Nothing. But he couldn't reach the back of the compartment.

Checking below to make sure he wasn't watched, Cooper carefully stepped onto the railing. He braced one hand against the wall and didn't look down as he balanced on the metal rail at the corner.

He peered into the hole, now below his natural eye level. Something was stuffed against the back of the dark compartment.

He wobbled slightly. Flattened his hand against the wall to brace himself.

He reached inside, pulled out…an envelope. Lance had left something.

Hope accelerated his heartbeat. This could be the edge they needed to—

His phone vibrated in his pocket. He carefully navigated down to the landing of the fire escape and pulled out his cell. "Bobby?"

"Hey, Coop. Got some news you're not gonna like."

"Yeah?"

"So my buddy I'm staying with while you crash at my place…"

Cooper stuffed the folded envelope into his waistband under his jacket while he waited for Bobby to get to the point. Which was probably that he wanted them out of his apartment sooner than he'd said.

"Well, he's into some stuff."

"What do you mean?"

"Like, stuff I didn't know about. Honest, I really didn't know he was, or I never would've picked him to stay with, you know?"

Cooper started to climb down the stairs of the fire escape. "Not really, Bobby. Can you get to the point?"

He laughed, a nervous laugh. Like when he'd done something stupid.

Cooper's pulse started to kick up. "Wait, what kind of stuff is he into?"

"Yeah, now you got the drift. He's hooked on snow, and he wants more. When he got high tonight, he told me his supplier was asking him about this lady with two-year-old twins they're looking for."

Cooper's heart banged into his ribs. He picked up his pace. Needed to find a taxi.

"Sounds like the whole cartel is looking for them. I was like, whoa. And I'm wondering, any chance that's who you're hiding from?"

"What did your friend tell the cartel, Bobby?"

"Well, this buddy of mine usually gets three when he tries to put two and two together, if you know what I mean, so I don't think he gave them anything they could use. But those kids are pretty cute. I wouldn't want…I just thought you should know."

Cooper waved at a taxi headed up the dark street. "Thanks, man."

"He knows where I live, Coop."

The taxi pulled to the curb as adrenaline surged into Cooper's veins. "Got it." He ducked into the taxi, praying he wouldn't be too late.

Valena stared at the door, ears straining to hear any sound.

Another creak.

The pressure of footsteps on the floor? Or just an old building.

She didn't want to be one of those females who lost it

every time a guy wasn't around. She'd lived alone most of the time for years. She could handle—

The doorknob wiggled.

Her breath seized in her throat, and she jerked away from the door. She went to the kitchen, swung a barstool to stand in front of the refrigerator. She stepped up on the stool and grabbed the Glock she'd put on top of the fridge to keep it out of the twins' reach.

Her gaze found the door.

Nothing. No sounds of someone trying to break in.

Maybe her fatigue was getting the best of her. How would the cartel or the DEA even know to come to this building, let alone this apartment? It could just be Cooper, looking for his key. She checked the digital clock of the microwave.

He'd said to expect him in another twenty minutes from now. And he had said they were safe here. He wouldn't have left otherwise, would he?

Reality slapped back the weak dependency of her question. Of course he would. She knew better than to depend on a man like him. The thirst for adventure was too much. He couldn't resist leaving for some nighttime op, never mind how vulnerable it left the twins.

A snap sounded from outside the door. Or the click of a gun being cocked? A safety removed?

A dog barked somewhere in the distance.

She dropped down from the stool, the Glock heavy in her hand.

Cooper had said to turn off the lights if she saw or heard anything suspicious. She probably should.

She took one step toward the light switch on the wall five feet away. She paused, listening for more signs something was truly wrong.

The DEA would knock, wouldn't they? And then they'd take the kids, Cooper had said.

But if it was the cartel…She held her breath. Maybe it wasn't either. Maybe it was only someone passing by. Quietly.

The silence was deafening, her heartbeat thudding in her ears the only sound she could hear.

She closed her grip around the handle of the gun and shifted the safety off. Her finger automatically found the trigger. Her dad had trained her to use a gun, but she'd never thought she would. Not on a person.

But she'd do it to protect her babies. She'd be ready.

The door smashed open.

A man in a black mask stood in the doorway, holding a gun.

She pulled the trigger, aiming to warn.

A pop sounded from the street outside.

CHAPTER
SEVENTEEN

COOPER PLUGGED the cartel's black SUV with a few more bullets.

The ducking driver crawled out the door on the other side, his booted feet visible under the belly of the vehicle. He had to be armed.

A flash flared with a pop from the rear of the SUV.

Cooper yanked back behind the corner of the building, crouching low.

Yep, definitely armed.

The cartel hadn't left guards at the getaway vehicle, which meant most of their muscle was in the building. They'd expected the fight there.

They should show up in about ten more seconds. If they didn't—

His chest clenched at the thought they might have already reached Valena and the twins. He'd heard a shot from the apartment right before he had first fired. *Please, God, keep them safe.*

Men in black masks and dark clothing spilled out of the apartment building in chaos. They ran behind the SUV, yelling things he couldn't make out. The driver would tell them where Cooper was.

Valena and the twins weren't with them.

Maybe he'd arrived in time. They would have instructions to keep the kids alive, so they shouldn't have hurt them and run.

Valena…

He pushed aside the distracting thought of her and accompanying pain in his chest. He needed to be ready for their counterattack.

The SUV wasn't leaving, though he intentionally hadn't hit anything vital, hoping they'd get scared and take off.

The feet of most of the men were visible on the other side of the SUV. They weren't running. Apparently more scared of whoever gave them orders than him.

Plan B.

He aimed, shot the mirror of the SUV.

The shatter drew out four men, positioned at each end of the SUV, crouched low into squats with their weapons drawn.

He shot into the windows of the SUV above their heads, aiming to keep them too busy ducking to return fire. Their stray bullets could hurt an innocent person in one of these apartment buildings.

Sirens sounded, not far away.

The cartel thugs apparently heard them, too. The four men disappeared behind the vehicle as the feet he could see underneath lifted, the men piling into the darkened SUV.

Their tires screeched as they pulled away.

Cooper drew back as they passed his corner, then watched as they took a turn, vanishing.

Plan B, complete.

He sprinted to the apartment building as the police sirens grew louder.

He prayed he'd find healthy twins and an unharmed, stubborn nanny.

The door opened.

Valena's hand stopped midway through stroking Savannah's hair. Hadn't they all gone? She got up from the edge of the bed and grabbed the gun off the nightstand.

"Valena?"

Cooper.

Her heart leaped, catapulted by a surge of relief.

"Valena?" His voice came closer.

"In the bedroom."

He appeared in the doorway, his handsome frame filling the space and making her pulse trip over itself. His gaze lit with fire as he watched her.

"The twins are fine. They're safe."

He glanced at the children in the bed, Sammy still sound asleep and Savannah's eyes drifting shut again.

He locked his gaze on her and walked into the room. He stopped in front of her, his eyes holding golden flecks, like the smoldering embers of the fire that was there a second ago. He stepped even closer, and his fingers gently touched her wrist.

A charge lit her skin and shot through her whole body as he cradled her wrist, his other hand taking the gun from her loosening grip.

"Are you all right?" His face, his lips, were so close, she could feel the breath of his whisper on her cheek.

She nodded, emotion squeezing her throat. She blinked back tears that suddenly fought to reach her eyes. She would not cry and go to pieces in front of him. This was his fault, after all.

She stepped back, and walked around him to the door. The

hallway felt cooler, like stepping into open air as she stalked to the living room.

"Valena." Cooper's voice behind her signaled he'd followed.

She whipped around to face him. "You said we'd be safe here."

The heat in his gaze cooled. "I didn't expect Bobby's friend to be connected with the cartel."

She folded her arms across her sweater. "You said you wanted me to trust you."

"I also told you to turn off the lights when I left, but they're all on."

"You told me to turn them off if I got suspicious someone was here."

He set the extra gun on the counter. "That's not what I said. But even if it was, don't you think five cartel thugs count as suspicious?"

"I only heard a tiny noise right before they kicked the door in." Her voice rose to a near shout. "Forgive me for forgetting to pack my X-ray goggles when you dragged us out of Florida in the middle of the night."

A soft cry came from the bedroom.

"Now look what you've done." She shot the words at Cooper as she brushed past him to the bedroom.

Savannah sat up in bed, whimpering and rubbing her eyes.

Valena lifted her, holding the girl close to her racing heart.

"I'm sorry."

She wasn't sure if it was the shock of the apology or Cooper's deep tone coming so close behind her that weakened her knees.

"Valena, I..." He sighed.

Without looking, she knew he was shoving his fingers across his hair, probably leaving a clump standing up that begged to be touched.

"I'm not used to…" His soft breath blew tendrils of her hair to brush her neck. "When I thought I might be too late, I got…scared. I guess I don't know how to handle that."

Scared? The soldier, special agent man, scared?

She turned to face him. The air whisked from her lungs at his proximity. She should be able to tell he was lying, but his gaze appeared as confused as her swirling mind. As if he wasn't sure what to do with the emotion she saw in his eyes.

Savannah sleepily let her head drop to Valena's shoulder, drawing Cooper's gaze.

His mouth softened into a curve, the small smile revealing tiny lines at the corners of his eyes. He reached to touch Savannah's blond curls, the warmth of his hand so near Valena's face leaving a trail of heat behind.

His gaze collided with hers. Was he remembering the moment earlier, when she thought he might have wanted to kiss her?

"We should go." His whisper was thick and raw.

Go. Again. The words threw a wet blanket on the flame that had sparked between them.

She pulled away. Always moving, always running. She couldn't keep putting the twins through this. "This has to stop."

"What?" His dark eyebrows lifted above a startled gaze.

A hot flush flooded her cheeks as she realized he might think she meant what had just passed between them. "I promised Miriam I would take care of the twins and give them a stable upbringing."

"You're doing the best you can. Miriam would understand. She'd be happy we care enough to keep the kids safe." He continued saying something about having to stay until the police left, but she barely heard him.

Was he right? Would Miriam have understood? Forgiven her for this? Because Valena sure couldn't. She'd made the same promise to herself. The twins would have all the security and stability she never had. They would have the attention they deserved. They would know they were loved.

Cooper drew her gaze as he gently lifted Sammy into his arms. The boy looked so small nestled against Cooper's chest, supported by his strong arms.

The image made her heart pump harder.

But a former soldier and DEA agent didn't have a clue how to give the twins what they really needed.

"You want this to stop?" Cooper held up a crumpled envelope in his hand. "Let's stop it."

CHAPTER
EIGHTEEN

THE PAPERS and flash drive from Lance's envelope lay neatly on the small table, like pieces of a puzzle waiting to be put together. If only they had a picture on a box to look at for the solution.

"You were right."

Valena glanced across the table at Cooper.

He smiled, his head turned to face the twins as they giggled, playing on the short slide of the fast-food restaurant's indoor playground. "This is good for them."

"They need a chance to be normal kids."

"Yeah." Cooper took another bite of his greasy breakfast sandwich.

She wrinkled her nose. "I don't know how you can eat that."

The twinkle in his eyes as he chewed made her stomach flip. "In my line of work, you never know when you're going to get the chance to eat. I never want to miss it."

She looked away from his disarming gaze, examining Lance's papers instead.

A scrap of paper had *City Mutual Bank East* and *City Mutual*

Bank Yorkville written in Lance's hurried scrawl, along with a list of specific weekdays and times.

Two computer print-outs featured a woman's photo and an employee profile from the City Mutual Bank website. Carissa Wulford, Chief Audit Executive.

"What does this all mean?"

Cooper wiped his mouth with a napkin. "I have an idea, but I'd like to see what's on the flash drive." He cast a glance at the notebook computer that sat open on the table.

The screen showed an icon as the computer tried to boot up.

He gave her a sideways smile. "I'm glad Bobby felt guilty enough to loan us his computer, but I really wish he had a newer one."

A squeal from the twins caught Valena's attention.

Sammy sat at the top of the slide, blocking Savannah.

Valena went to deal with the situation, coming back as soon as she had redirected the twins to various-sized balls to play with.

Cooper had the flash drive in the computer when she returned. "Got it." He angled the computer so she could see the screen, as well.

A single folder appeared, labeled *Violet.*

Valena's nerves tingled.

Cooper clicked on the folder, and a password protection box popped onto the screen. "No surprise. He locked it." But a frown still pulled at Cooper's mouth. He turned his gaze to Valena. "Any ideas?"

"For his password? No."

"It must be something he was sure one of us would know."

She thought hard. "Maybe a date? Like Miriam's birthday or the date they were married?"

"Too obvious. And anyone could get that kind of information." Cooper typed in those dates anyway, but both failed. "What about something Lance said to you...something he said pretty often."

Her gaze drifted toward the twins as she wracked her brain. Morning sunlight poured through the floor-to-ceiling windows, casting a glow on their blond hair.

Angels.

"Twin Angels." She swung her head to Cooper. "That's what he called the twins. Could that be it?"

Cooper's fingers flew over the keys as he typed it in.

Failed.

"I'll try without caps." He typed in several more variations. "Nope. I think it's too straightforward. He would've used numbers or something." A smile shot light to Cooper's eyes. "I've got it." His hands hovered over the keyboard to type again. "Angels, squared. With a two and a *d*."

The password box disappeared, and the folder opened to reveal a long list of files.

"Good call." She leaned in to see the documents on the screen. "What are those?"

He opened several of the files, each one a similarly formatted document with numbers.

"Bank statements?"

"Looks like it. From City Mutual Bank."

"Why would he have collected these?" She glanced at Cooper. Goodness, his face was close.

Lines crossed his forehead and his eyebrows pulled together as he concentrated on the screen.

Which she should be doing, too, instead of getting distracted by his adorable expression. She forced her gaze back to the computer.

"Some of these accounts are the same, and some are different." Cooper pointed at the bottom of a document. "Look at the transaction numbers." He clicked through a few more as she watched the transaction records. "Some of the deposits made to one account are exactly the same as a deposit to another of these accounts the day before."

"You're right." She looked at the dates listed to see what he'd spotted. The record also showed the days of the week and times. She'd seen some of them before. "Wait."

"What?"

She grabbed Lance's scrap of paper and moved it in front of the computer. "These days and times are the same as those big deposits. See?" She checked the information on the screen against Lance's list. "Third Thursday at two fifteen p.m. First Tuesday at nine forty-five a.m."

"Good work, Valena." The excitement in Cooper's voice prompted her heart to beat faster. He checked more documents until there was no doubt about the pattern of large deposits, always over $100,000, matching Lance's list.

"So what are those deposits?"

"I'd bet anything they're drug money. Drop-offs."

"At a bank?"

"Sure."

She leaned back against the chair. "You mean drug dealers can just take their dirty money to a bank and deposit it without anyone noticing?"

"Well, they probably have someone who doesn't look like a dealer make the deposit. A good bank should get suspicious at large amounts of cash being deposited so regularly, but there's usually an employee who will look the other way for the right price."

Valena glanced at the twins, who had returned to the slide, then brought her gaze back to Cooper. "But why would they put money in a bank in the first place? I thought they just kept it and used it."

"Cash is highly traceable and suspicious, especially in large amounts." He folded his arms on the table in front of him, the sinews of his muscled forearms showing beneath the pushed-up sleeves of his black sweater. "There's no safe way to get it to the kingpin of the cartel in Columbia without leaving a trail for either our government or theirs. But if they can get the cash into the accounts of dummy corporations made to look legit, the money becomes another reasonable-looking number on a computer screen."

"But the bank branches on Lance's list are here in Chicago. The cartel is in Florida."

Cooper leveled a gaze at her. "You've seen the evidence of their Chicago presence. They started in Florida, but they've spread across the country. Large cities like Chicago are especially rich for them." His head jerked to the entrance.

A middle-aged woman with a boy about twelve entered the restaurant and went to the counter.

Cooper had reacted the same way to every one of the few people who came in at five a.m., even the two elderly men who'd sat in the back corner by the restrooms. But given how much the image of the masked man in the apartment doorway still haunted Valena, she didn't mind his vigilance at the moment.

He swung his attention back to her. "I'm guessing Lance came with the cartel to Chicago undercover, and that's when he found this." Cooper gestured to the open documents on the screen. "No wonder he was excited. This is big."

Not big enough to warrant putting the twins in danger.

Cooper's gaze rested on her face, as if he saw her skepticism. "Money laundering is a huge part of keeping the drug trade going. If we can stop the cartel from cleaning their dirty money, we could end their business on our turf." His dark eyes shimmered.

"You're excited, too."

A grin widened his mouth. "There's nothing better than knowing you're doing something that makes a difference. If we can finish this, we'll save potentially thousands of lives—the people who OD, those murdered because of the drug running, not to mention people who aren't really living at all because of their addiction." Passion fired his eyes as he leaned forward.

A reminder of why she'd better not let herself get attached to him. He was born for this kind of work. Like her dad. Cooper wasn't the family man type. Even if he wasn't under the thumb of the government anymore, he was a soldier on a mission. And he always would be.

She looked at Sammy and Savannah. "And the twins and I could go home."

Silence greeted her statement.

She risked a glance.

"Right." The glimmer had vanished from his eyes. "You'd all be safe."

They both looked away.

The sound of crinkling signaled Cooper crumpling up his sandwich wrap and shoving it in the brown bag it had come in. "That guy outside just lit his third cigarette."

She started to turn her head. "What—"

Cooper's hand on hers halted the question. "Don't look." His dark eyes were a contrast of calm to her racing pulse. Which better have nothing to do with the warm sensation of his hand covering hers on the table.

"Act normal and gather the twins as calmly as you can."

She swallowed as he pulled his hand away.

He sent the man a surreptitious glance so quickly she wasn't sure he had checked at all. "The smoker just sent a text to someone. We have to leave now."

▭

Cooper slung the backpack that housed the computer over one shoulder and looked directly at the smoker as they exited the McDonald's.

The young guy turned the other direction, the hood of his gray sweatshirt hiding his head.

Cooper followed Valena onto the blacktop of the parking lot, Sammy toddling along at her side while Savannah waved at Cooper over Valena's shoulder.

Cooper smiled and waved back, then checked over his shoulder.

The smoker jerked his head away from watching them but stayed on the sidewalk along the building as a car passed to enter the drive-through.

He was either waiting for Cooper to let down his guard, or the guy wasn't ready to act on his own. Which would mean the text, if that was what he'd typed into his phone, would bring friends.

Valena glanced at their observer as she stopped by the side door of the van. "Looks like an ordinary kid to me."

"Probably is." Cooper unlocked the door and slid it open, dropping the backpack on the floor inside. "Up you go, buddy." He lifted Sammy into the van and set him on the floor before quickly checking for the smoker.

Still loitering in the same spot.

"You can't expect me to believe he's DEA." Valena's mouth held a tense line.

"Too obvious for DEA." He swept his hand toward the van, indicating she should get Savannah in.

Valena rolled her eyes as she stepped up into the van. "Not everyone is hooked on drugs or into violence, you know." She set Savannah in the car seat and started to strap her in.

Cooper angled so he could see Valena in the van and the smoker at the same time. "True."

"But you're still standing there like a bodyguard instead of helping with the twins." She bent to grab Sammy as he tried to trot away.

A smile tugged at Cooper's lips despite the cartel lackey hovering. "I thought you didn't need any help."

"Cute." The glare she shot him said she wasn't seeing the humor. She finished securing Sammy into his car seat and stepped down from the van. Her gaze followed Cooper's to the smoker. "Couldn't he just be a guy with a smoking problem?"

The lackey left the sidewalk, giving them a wide berth and looking at his phone as he crossed to a parked gray two-door five stalls away.

"Get in." Cooper reached past Valena to close the door.

For once, she didn't argue and headed around the van to the passenger side as he sat behind the wheel.

"If he were with the cartel, wouldn't he already have tried to take the kids?" She slid into the passenger seat as he started the engine.

Cooper shoved the car in reverse and backed out of the stall, keeping the gray car in view. "I don't think he's cartel himself. We know from Bobby that the cartel spread the word about us already. If a user like Bobby's friend knows, anybody who's bought heroin in the Chicago area could notice us and call it in."

The gray car stayed put as Cooper drove to exit the parking lot.

"But why would other people want to hurt us?"

He glanced at her. "It's not personal. They were likely promised free dope for info." He swung the van onto the road.

Valena let out a sigh, turning her head to watch the parking lot.

"So far so good. He's not moving." Cooper kept a close eye on the mirrors in case the guy peeled out of the parking lot. "And no company. Yet."

"You really love this stuff, don't you?" She'd brought her attention back to him, her violet gaze on his face. "I can see it in your eyes. They light up every time we're in danger or when you talk about getting the cartel."

He swallowed, suddenly feeling like he was in the witness stand at a trial. "I guess in a way I do."

"Good to see the fire in your eyes again." Jenkin's observation as they had escaped the DEA in his jeep rang in Cooper's mind. *"Business must be picking up."*

But business hadn't picked up or become anything more than pointless. Until the cartel broke into Lance's house. Until he'd extracted Valena and the twins and gotten them to safety. Then the DEA showing up at the cottage...He'd almost forgotten what adrenaline felt like. What doing something that mattered felt like. Lance was on to something huge and important. It could save so many lives.

But he hadn't enjoyed the way his heart had wrenched when Valena screamed in the cabin, or the agony of wondering if the cartel would beat him to the apartment and—

He cleared his throat. "I like having a purpose and feeling like I'm doing something good in the world. That I'm helping people. But seeing you and the twins in danger..." He briefly looked into those beautiful eyes, his chest tightening. "There's nothing to like about that."

He had to pull his gaze away to look at the road. Check the mirror.

A black SUV lurked behind them.

Energy surged through his body. "We've got company." And for how long before he'd seen them? He could kick himself for getting distracted. He scanned the road ahead and the two-lane street running perpendicular at the upcoming intersection. He was familiar with the suburb. Should be able to lose them. *Help me lose them, Lord.*

He gauged the distance between them and the intersection where the light turned red. "Hang on."

"There are children in the van, Cooper." Valena's voice was tight, but strong as always.

"I'll keep them safe. But I can't promise they'll enjoy the ride." He pressed the pedal to the floor.

CHAPTER
NINETEEN

"IT'S OKAY, baby. We'll get you all cleaned up." Valena leaned over Savannah's car seat in the back of the van, using wipes to clean up the last of the vomit.

"Yucky?" Savannah's big blue eyes captured Valena's gaze. The girl sat on the bench seat, her smooth ivory skin a shade paler than normal.

"Yes, it was yucky, but I'm getting it all cleaned up."

"What that?" Sammy craned his head to watch the process from his car seat as he asked his favorite question for the fourth time since they'd stopped at the gas station.

"Savannah was sick, honey."

"Do you need more wipes?"

Valena straightened as much as she could under the low ceiling and looked at Cooper.

"I could go back in and get some." Angled toward them in the driver's seat, his gaze rested on Savannah. "Or maybe I could get her some medicine or something?"

"No. We have enough wipes. But I won't be able to get her completely clean without a bath. And somewhere to wash and dry her clothes."

"Will she be okay?" Remorse and compassion swirled in the dark gaze he aimed at Valena.

Her heart squeezed. She'd never seen a man so concerned about a child. Somehow she couldn't be mad at him when he looked at her like that. "She'll be fine. She's gotten sick in the car before, once when I just drove them to the grocery store. She's always been prone to motion sickness."

Some of the pain in his eyes receded as he looked at Savannah, but worried lines still crossed his forehead.

Valena turned back to Savannah, squatting down in front of her to clean a spot of vomit off her yellow cotton pants. "You kept us safe and lost the cartel. That's the important thing."

When he didn't respond, she looked over her shoulder to see his face.

The surprise in his expression faded as his gaze caught hers, pulling her into a rich pool of warmth.

She could drown in those depths. But she'd better not. She made herself turn away and focus on the task of getting Savannah into her car seat. *Keep your distance.* Or distance was all she'd have left if she fell for a guy like him.

"So what do we do next?" She kept her back to him as she buckled Savannah in.

"We'll need to ditch the van. The cartel knows it, and the DEA is bound to know what we're driving by now, too."

She risked a glance his way. "You think the DEA is still trying to find us, too?"

"Count on it. They're more strategic than the cartel. The longer we don't see them, the more worried I get."

She turned to face him as tension squeezed her belly. Could be Cooper just imagining the worst. But his suspicions hadn't been wrong so far.

"We'll be fine. Fortunately, I know the way the agents think.

They can't predict our next move because we're running down Lance's intel. And we know he didn't share it with them because of the leak. So they're flying blind, trying to catch up to us." He smiled, but his serious gaze didn't lighten like usual. "As long as they can't predict where we'll go next, we should be good."

"But the cartel?"

"They might know what Lance found. They might be able to guess where we'll look next. But they might not know the details." His lips tightened at the corners. "We'll have to hope they don't."

Her pulse sped up in response to his less-than-confident statement. At least he was being honest. That was an improvement.

He pulled back as she approached the middle console and climbed over it to reach the front passenger seat.

"You're right."

She looked at him as she sat down. He was actually admitting she was right about something?

"We need to end this. And I think I know how."

Hope stirred in the pool of nerves occupying her stomach. "From Lance's evidence?"

"Well, that's just it, it's not evidence—not the hard, indisputable kind he'd need to make a solid case against anyone." Cooper tapped his long fingers against the steering wheel. "He probably had to go back to Columbia to keep his cover and couldn't get the evidence he needed from there. At least not soon enough."

"So we need more than what we have? The times and days the drug money is deposited and then shows up in supposedly legitimate business accounts isn't enough?"

"Catching a small fish like the bribed bank employee or the messenger with the money wouldn't hurt the cartel. Lance was aiming for a big fish."

The photo of the Chief Audit Executive sprang up in Valena's memory. "Carissa Wulford."

"Exactly. As the head of the auditing department, she'd be in the perfect position to manipulate accounts and transfer deposits to offshore accounts easily, without needing to fear anyone noticing."

"That's why Lance had her picture in the envelope."

Cooper nodded, the spark of energy back in his eyes. "Has to be. He said the answer wasn't where he thought. Because it was here in the U.S., not Columbia. When the DEA mole fingered Lance, the cartel must've learned he had found something. By grabbing the twins, they could lure Lance to them, find out what evidence he had, and destroy it along with him."

Her stomach churned. "And the children."

Cooper's dark gaze softened. "That won't happen. Especially now that we have Lance's lead. If we can take out the head of the U.S. money laundering operation, we'll end the threat to the twins and kill the cartel's business within our borders."

"But you said there's no way to tie this woman to the evidence Lance collected."

Cooper shook his head. "Those transactions all had different employees listed. She must log in to different employees' accounts each time she moves the money around in order to cover her tracks."

"Smart."

"Yeah. But nobody's perfect. We need to figure out where she's vulnerable."

"And then?"

"Then we finish what Lance started."

"Eat me?" Sammy's small voice drifted between them from the back seat.

A smile curved Cooper's mouth. "He just ate."

Valena shrugged one shoulder, an answering smile on her lips. "He's a boy."

Cooper chuckled, the deep sound sending a tingle through her diaphragm. He started the engine, casting a grin her way that for some ridiculous reason made her pulse flutter. "First things first, get the twins and their nanny someplace safe with food, bathtub, and a washer and dryer."

She looked away, staring at nothing out the passenger window as he drove the van from the parking lot. Her heart pumped erratically beneath her ribs.

She gripped the handle of the door with her fingers. Because at this moment, keeping her distance from Cooper was the last thing she wanted to do.

___

Cooper shifted on the too-firm sofa and flipped to the next page of the Gideon Bible he'd found in the drawer of the hotel room. But the words blurred beneath the image of Valena's genuine surprise when she'd learned that he prayed.

"Men like you don't want anything to lean on. Or anyone."

He could be making calls or searching for information on Carissa Wulford while he waited for Valena to finish bathing the twins. Instead, her remark wouldn't leave him alone. Maybe because he'd been so hypocritical in his response, telling her to start praying herself.

But she was right.

Before the twins and Valena were nearly taken, he hadn't been praying and hadn't cracked open his Bible in longer than he wanted to admit. Prayer and Bible reading had become far too frustrating...almost seemed pointless after Gillian left him. God just didn't seem to care.

"All clean and..."

Cooper looked up to see Valena holding Savannah, the

girl's blond curls darkened and tousled with water. Then he realized Valena was staring. At the Bible in his hands.

She brought her gaze up to his, raising her eyebrows.

"What?" A defensive note crept into his voice.

"I just didn't take you for a—"

"Christian?" Irritation infused the word. Why should she judge him for it?

"I was going to say reader." She pressed her lips together. "You're a Christian?"

"You say it like that's a bad thing."

Her violet eyes darkened to deeper purple. Probably thanks to the edge of his tone. "My mom believes in God. Never helped her." She spun on her heel and returned to the bathroom.

Cooper pushed up from the sofa, leaving the Bible on the coffee table as he followed her. He leaned against the open doorway.

She set Savannah down and squatted to towel dry Sammy's hair, the boy sitting on the lid of the closed toilet.

The scene looked so sweet and idyllic—a mother affectionately caring for her little ones.

A lump clogged his throat. Before he could start imagining himself as the father and husband, he pushed out the words he'd followed her to say. "I'm sorry I got so defensive."

She paused the drying for a second. Then continued, not looking his way.

"Why do you say your mom's faith never helped her?"

She lowered the towel and slowly stood. "She did all the religious things. She's Catholic, and for as long as I can remember, she's always gone to every mass, said her prayers, never spoken a bad word."

Valena dropped the wet towel on a pile of others on the floor, then pushed the pile into the corner.

Cooper waited. Hoped she'd open the window to her soul he sensed had just been cracked.

"The harder things got with Dad, the more candles she would light at church." Valena turned toward him. Hurt filled her eyes despite her rueful smile.

His heart pinched painfully at the sight.

"Just like the candles we would put on the table when we set it for dinner every night, waiting for Dad to get home." She crossed her arms over her sweater. "Those stupid candles. I don't know why she kept trying, why she didn't tell me the truth and tell me to stop hoping. He never showed when we wanted him to." Anger flared in her eyes. "Neither did God."

Cooper's mouth tasted dry. He wanted to answer, to tell her God was there. That she didn't have to light candles to draw near to Him or access His comfort. That God had a purpose in those sad times.

But hypocrisy bound his tongue. Hadn't he blamed God for letting Gillian dump him for another guy? For letting him think he was going to get the family he'd always dreamed of having, only to shatter the dream in such a painful way?

Part of him still blamed God, despite the twinge of guilt that came with the inward admission. God did seem distant, just as Valena described.

"I'm sorry." The whisper was all he could manage, with a heart full of remorse, guilt, and regret. And a heart desperate to shield her from more pain.

CHAPTER
TWENTY

A NERVOUS SENSATION twisted Valena's stomach, making her wish she hadn't eaten the Cobb salad at the family-style restaurant. She stared at herself in the mirror of the restaurant's public restroom as she washed her hands.

Her skin was paler than normal, and bags had formed under her eyes. Makeup hardly seemed to matter while running from criminals who wanted to kidnap her babies. But she could only imagine what Cooper must be thinking when he looked at her.

She pushed aside the schoolgirl thought. Who cared what he thought? The more unattractive she looked, the better. The last thing she needed was an adventure junkie like Cooper getting ideas.

She blew out a breath and shook the excess water from her hands before going to the paper towel dispenser on the wall.

They had a plan now. Cooper had already figured out where Carissa Wulford lived and deduced she'd have to use her home computer for her illegal transactions to avoid being caught by the bank's employee monitoring system.

This would all soon be over. Valena dropped the used

towels in the trash and pulled open the door of the ladies' restroom. All they—

She slammed into something solid.

A man's chuckle and his hands on her arms made her jolt back, heart pounding. "Take it easy, Valena. I won't hurt you."

She'd never seen the thin man with red hair and green eyes before. But she knew that voice.

He flipped open an ID wallet, a smirk on his chapped lips. "Agent Hinds, at your service."

She crossed her arms to hide her racing heartbeat. Was Cooper still with the twins at the table? She couldn't see them from this back hallway. Which could be good. Had Hinds' seen them?

"You seem nervous, Valena."

The slippery salesman way he said her name made her stomach churn even more.

"No need to be. I'm not here for the children." His smile froze as he stared at her. "Yet."

"Then what do you want?" She got the question out in a strong tone. She would not be intimidated by a government puppet. It could be her dad standing in front of her.

The thought infused her with irritation, slowing her heart rate to a steady pace more fitting this ridiculous attempt to intimidate her. If Hinds hadn't made a move on the children, that meant he couldn't for some reason. Probably a superior had tied his hands.

"We want your cooperation."

She nearly rolled her eyes at his switch to the governmental *we*. "And why in the world would you expect to get that? I suggest you come up with a much better reason than you did on the phone."

"Oh, I have." His gaze followed a woman who entered the hallway, giving them a curious glance as she passed by.

Valena didn't dare try to use the woman's presence as a way out.

Hinds no doubt had a gun under his jacket and the badge to use it.

Once the woman disappeared into the restroom, he returned his gaze to Valena. "White has no doubt informed you that we have it in our power to take the children from your custody."

She didn't need to think of her dad to get angry now. Her blood heated, making her itch to wipe the puppet's smile off his face.

"Good, I'm glad you don't deny it. Now I personally have no desire to separate you and the children."

She glared at him. For some reason, he apparently thought she was stupid enough to believe him.

"I can personally guarantee the children will remain with you if you agree to give us the information we need about White."

She blinked. "What information?"

"We need to know what he's doing. We know he was in contact with Acker before he disappeared and seems to be working with him now in Chicago. What is he up to?"

"Why do you think I would tell you anything?"

"Well, aside from wanting to keep the children, I would think you wouldn't want to aid and abet a criminal."

"Criminal?"

The agent's eyes gleamed. "Your friends White and Acker are likely working for the cartel."

She let out a snort, lowering her arms. "Are you insane? You clearly don't know Cooper at all. Or Lance."

A flash lit his gaze, but he doused it quickly. "Very well." The nauseating smile gave way to a firmly set jaw as he took a step toward her. "I'll tell you the truth."

As if he knew the meaning of the word. "Please do."

"We suspect White and Acker may be working together to engage in money laundering. With drug profits, no less."

"Wha—"

"We believe they've gotten hold of drug money and are trying to move it off shore where they can access it without being apprehended."

She tried not to let surprise show on her face. Could Hinds know about the illegal activity at City Mutual?

"Your silence is quite incriminating. We know White visited a bank headquarters today, pretending to be a securities advisor."

"That's not..." She stopped short of telling him Cooper had done that to find out if they had a monitoring system on employees' computers. Hinds was only trying to trick her.

He moved even closer, looking down at her with cool green eyes. "Think about it, Miss Greer. Has White been honest with you from the beginning? Do you really know why he's risking his life and is unwilling to let the children out of his reach? He knows the cartel will use them to turn Lance against him."

She took a step back, shaking her head. "You're wrong." Wasn't he?

"You can help us find out the truth. I need you to tell me what information White has from Acker and what he's planning to do with it." His lips flatlined when she didn't respond. "I'll give you twelve hours to choose to do your duty for your country. And for those children. Their future is at stake." He spun away and left the hallway.

She tried to wait until she'd calmed, but she had to see her babies. She stepped out of the hallway, her gaze darting to the table where she'd left them with Cooper.

They were there.

Breath returned to her lungs.

Hinds was nowhere in sight.

She made her way to the table as Cooper gently wiped Savannah's jam-covered hands with a napkin and said something to Sammy.

Cooper looked up when she approached, but she avoided his gaze, sitting down and grabbing the nearest glass of water. "Everything okay?"

How did he know something was wrong so quickly? She forced a smile. "Sure. Fine. I'm just tired."

What she felt wasn't fatigue. Part of her wanted to tell Cooper everything that had happened. But she felt as if Hinds' gaze was boring into her back. He could be watching her right now. Maybe listening to what she said somehow.

But it wasn't really fear that pinned her tongue. It was a hovering, growing doubt. A dark question cloaking her mind. What if Hinds was right?

▭

"I've never done surveillance with two-year-olds before." Cooper rotated his head to see Valena in the back of the rented car, wedged between the twins' car seats.

She gave him only a weak smile for his effort to lighten the mood.

He frowned as he turned back to look out the windshield, his gaze returning to the view of Carissa Wulford's luxury home. But his mind stayed on Valena. Something had been bothering her ever since she'd left to use the bathroom at the restaurant. She'd taken a long time, and her cheeks were pale when she'd returned to the table.

He didn't want to be tactless if the stress was making her sick or something. But his suspicions only grew with her silence. And the way she'd jerk her gaze away every time he looked at her, as if she'd been watching him. From the firm set of her mouth and the coldness in her eyes, she wasn't watching for the reason he might hope.

Had someone gotten to her? Scared her somehow behind his back?

He narrowed his eyes at the house, though nothing there had changed except the fading light as sunset drew near.

Valena wouldn't cooperate with the cartel, would she? No. She was too smart and loved the twins too much to do anything for those thugs. But coercion wasn't the cartel's style anyway.

It was the DEA's. Especially Hinds'.

Cooper thought back to the restaurant. Could Hinds have slipped past him somehow to get to her? Cooper hadn't gone to the bathrooms himself. Maybe there was a rear exit. Or maybe he'd been too preoccupied with the twins to be as alert as he should have. He'd relaxed, knowing the public setting afforded them protection from the cartel and probably the DEA. Stupid lapse in judgment.

He glanced at Valena in the mirror.

A genuine smile tilted her lips as she tickled Sammy, and he giggled wildly.

His heart squeezed. Would she let Hinds trick her into doing something stupid? He opened his mouth to question her. Closed it.

They'd been getting along better. Working together. He had hoped she might be starting to trust him. He could destroy that by assuming the worst.

He'd wait. As long as he could. And hope she would come to him on her own. That she'd choose to trust him enough to tell him what had happened.

"How long do we have to watch her house?" Valena's gaze was on him through the mirror. Could she tell what he'd been thinking?

He looked at the house. "Just till dark. I already know her

security system's a joke. She should've gone with Warren instead of the Dark Protect system. We never use it because of the fatal vulnerabilities."

His gaze moved to the garage door that hadn't opened again since Wulford had pulled her Beemer inside. "She's apparently home at night but gone to work during the day. So the safest time for me to bypass the security system will be in the morning after she leaves."

"So tomorrow?"

"I wish we had more time for surveillance to make sure of her Thursday schedule, but..." He caught Valena's gaze in the mirror. "I know it's important we move fast."

She looked away. "Very."

"So we'll make our move tomorrow."

"We?"

He tried to smile. "Of course. We're in this together, right?"

She stared at him, conflicting emotions he couldn't pin down crossing her face. "You're sure this will work?"

"Don't you trust me?" The words slipped out before he could catch them.

She pulled her gaze away, using Savannah's whine as an excuse.

His throat tightened for no good reason. This plan had better work. He needed to hurry up and get the kids safely back where they belonged while his heart was still safe, too.

"I'LL ENTER HERE."

"The front door?" Valena stared at the blueprints of Carissa Wulford's house that Cooper had laid out on the coffee table in front of the sofa where they sat.

He nodded. "I'll have disabled the security system, so going in at the front of the house will actually look less suspicious to any neighbor who might be watching. They'll assume I have a key or someone let me in."

She barely heard his answer. Hinds had given her twelve hours to make her decision. Only about three more hours to go.

Would he find her somehow? Or just show up and take the twins if she didn't agree to be his spy?

"The housekeeper comes on Fridays and there are no pets, so the house should be empty."

She watched Cooper's hand as his tanned finger traced the path from the front door to the home office.

"I'll be able to reach the office in less than ten seconds and get to her computer. Installing the software could take five to seven minutes, depending on the speed of her computer."

Valena's gaze drifted from his strong hand up his sweater-clad arm to his trim jawline and dark eyelashes.

Could he be lying to her about everything? Using her to get the drug money for himself? She knew Lance well enough to know he wouldn't do such a thing—certainly not at risk of his own children. Then again, she never would have believed Lance was a special agent for the government either.

Her stomach cinched even tighter than it had been for the past couple hours. At least the children were safe and asleep in real beds in the separate bedroom of this hotel suite. But could she keep them safe if Cooper was fooling her?

He abruptly turned his head toward her.

She hadn't realized they were sitting so close, his face now only inches away. She felt the heat from his body and the disarming impact of his gaze as he looked into her eyes.

"Will you tell me what's wrong?" Concern softened his eyes to a melting chocolate. Could he look at her like that if he was conning her?

She opened her mouth to give her auto, safe response, but he touched a finger to her lips.

"Don't say you're fine." His words were a husky whisper. A smile tugged at his mouth as he lowered his finger, slowly, like he didn't want to. "Those eyes. They show so much."

Her heart thumped erratically against her ribs, but she couldn't pull her gaze from his.

"Something's bothering you. Since the restaurant. Something upset you. What is it?"

She searched his soft brown eyes. "I didn't think it mattered if we were upset. We just have to stay alive and get the job done."

"Oh, it matters." His gaze roved over her face, coming to rest on her eyes.

The emotion in his gaze sucked the breath from her lungs.

It was something beyond just caring. Something stronger. It was similar to what she'd seen in his eyes when Savannah had gotten sick in the van. Or when he'd said he was sorry for what Valena had gone through with her dad. As if he was absorbing her pain, the children's pain. As if he wanted desperately to end it, to help, to protect her and the twins. And he'd done his best to do just that since he'd rescued them from the house in Florida.

No, he couldn't be up to anything but trying to end this nightmare and bring down the cartel.

She took a deep breath. "Hinds caught me by the restrooms."

Cooper's eyes darkened, his hands closing on her upper arms. "Did he threaten you? Hurt you?"

She shook her head. "No. He wanted me to agree to spy for him. On you."

Cooper dropped his grip and stood, stalking toward the window where moonlight pushed through the thin curtain.

She got to her feet, barely resisting the urge to go after him and apologize. "He said you and Lance are planning to take the cartel money yourselves. So he wanted me to tell him what information you have and what you're doing with it."

Cooper kept his back to her. "You believed him?"

Her heart twisted. Would he hate her for doubting him? "I didn't know what to believe."

He turned to face her, pain of his own reflected in his eyes. "Do you now?"

Her pulse tripped. "I think so."

He took two steps toward her. Paused. "I'm sorry I let him get past me. I left you vulnerable."

Her heart melted. He wasn't mad at her. And he was trying to take the blame on himself. "You can't be everywhere all the time."

He moved closer, stopping only inches in front of her. He touched her hands, dangling at her sides, and took her fingers gently in his. His intense gaze looked deeply into hers as his voice dropped to a whisper. "Thank you for trusting me."

Warmth traveled from her chest down to her toes. She did trust him. And it didn't scare her. In fact, his proximity and his strong hands gingerly cradling hers had quite the opposite effect.

His gaze dropped to her mouth.

A jolt shot through her system, and her heart raced. Was he going to kiss her?

He lowered his head to hers.

She closed her eyes, felt his lips touch the corner of her mouth.

She opened her eyes as he pulled away, drawing in a ragged breath.

He backed up, releasing her hands, as she stared at him in confusion. "You'd better get some sleep while you can."

She blinked at him. What had just happened? Was he having second thoughts about her because she'd doubted him? "Okay." She pushed the word past her dry mouth. She turned to go to the bedroom but paused in the doorway. The twins slept soundly in one full-size bed and the other stood empty.

She turned back to Cooper.

He still stood by the sofa, watching her with that intense gaze.

"You don't have to sleep on the sofa this time, you know. There are two beds. I'll share with the twins anyway."

A smile curved his lips. "I better stay out here."

"Oh. You mean for safety?" He must want to keep watch for the cartel.

His smile slid into an ironic angle. "Something like that."

The heat in his eyes made her realize what he meant. And why he hadn't given her a real kiss.

Her cheeks warmed as she looked away. No, she wasn't sorry she trusted this man. In fact, her heart might be about to take a much bigger leap than that.

She turned back to the bedroom.

Just as the window shattered.

TWENTY-TWO

BULLETS PEPPERED the room as Cooper dove onto Valena, pulling her to the ground and covering her body with his own.

"The twins!" She squirmed under him.

"They're aiming for us." He kept her pinned for her own safety. "They won't hurt the kids." He prayed he was right.

The gunfire stopped. For a moment.

"Stay down." He took the risk of rolling off her. Crawled to the opening where the window used to be, angling away from shattered pieces of glass.

More shots sprayed the room.

He pressed against the wall, lifting his Glock from its holster.

Valena dropped to the floor, apparently having stood when he'd told her not to.

"Stay down." Stubborn woman.

Another smatter of bullets.

He slid his head closer to the window.

A spark of light flashed in the opened window of a dark room across the street when more shots flew. Far enough the shooter could miss and hit the kids. And the automatic weapon the shooter was using clearly wasn't intended to aim precisely.

Crying started in the bedroom.

More shots.

He looked out the window. If he could pinpoint the shooter, he could return fire. But these were apartment buildings. He didn't want to risk hitting the wrong pers—

Movement in the bedroom doorway caught his eye.

Savannah walked into view, crying.

Valena jumped up and ran to the girl.

Shots popped.

He whirled and fired out the window into the room across the street.

Silence.

Savannah began to cry again, softly.

"Valena?" He couldn't see her or Savannah past the sofa.

No response.

His heart froze. Was she shot?

He tested moving partially in front of the window.

No bullets.

Police sirens sounded in the distance.

The shooter had likely left.

Either way, he had to risk moving to check on Valena. He went the long way around the room, but no shots went off.

His shoes crunched over the glass scattered across the room as he scanned for Valena. She wasn't by the sofa. Had she made it into the bedroom?

He went to the doorway.

Sammy still lay in bed, sleeping. The boy really could sleep through anything.

More crying drew his gaze to the floor just inside the door.

Valena sat with her back to the wall, clutching Savannah in her arms.

His breath returned even as an ache squeezed his chest at the sight of her. Blood streaked her hand. "Valena."

She lifted those gorgeous violet eyes to his face.

His heart thumped. "You're hurt."

She shook her head, but the blood he spotted running along her neck, creeping out from under her hair called her a liar.

A hot rush of anger mixed with concern surged up his throat, threatening to choke him. How could he have let his guard down like that? The cartel had figured out where they were and saw they had a chance of eliminating the guardians to get at the twins. And he'd practically set them out on a platter.

He went to the bathroom and grabbed two neatly folded washcloths off the counter. He shoved them under the faucet, clenching his jaw. This was why he shouldn't get personally involved with the people he needed to protect. He knew that. But he'd ignored that rule and made Valena and the twins vulnerable because he was too distracted to do his job. He shouldn't have let them come back to the same hotel room twice in one day. He should have been watching for danger instead of talking to Valena.

He'd gotten emotionally involved. And Valena got hurt.

He returned to her with the damp washcloths and squatted down.

Savannah's crying had quieted to a whimper as she rested her head on Valena's shoulder.

"Savannah."

She lifted her head to look at Cooper.

"It's okay, baby girl." He used the warm cloth to wipe the tears and spatter of blood off Savannah's small cheeks and forehead. "There, there." Thank the Lord, washing didn't reveal any actual cuts. Which meant the blood was all Valena's.

A lump lodged in his throat, but he smiled at Savannah as he touched her round chin with his finger. "Can't have my girl in distress, can I?"

A hint of a dawning smile lit Savannah's pretty blue eyes.

He looked at Valena, catching a glimmer of moisture in the gaze that watched him. Was she in pain?

He swallowed. "Now for my other girl." He shouldn't say that, but his pounding heart couldn't be denied. He reached to push back her soft hair.

She shook her head, the hair falling forward over the blood. "I'm fine." She met his gaze, pain reflected in her eyes. But she still refused help.

She was the most stubborn and exasperating woman he'd ever met. Also the toughest.

"You'll get blood on the twins." He reached to move the hair again, and this time she let him.

Her eyes half closed, doing murder to his pulse as he cleaned the blood off her neck, careful to avoid the cut that cleaning revealed. He breathed more evenly when he saw the cut wasn't as large as he had feared. He couldn't see any glass imbedded in it. "I don't think you'll need stiches."

"Of course I won't need stiches. Just put a bandage on it, and I'll be fine."

"Yes, ma'am." He stood and turned away before she could see his smile. He went to the backpack he'd stuffed a first aid kit into back at the cottage.

He'd never met a woman like her. Gillian would probably be going to pieces right about now. Not that she'd have ever cared enough about someone else's children to put herself in danger for them. But she wouldn't have liked him getting mixed up in something like this either.

Quitting the DEA for her was supposed to mean no more adventures. No more traveling or danger. That had certainly been true. Until now. But could he have prevented this altogether if he'd never left the DEA?

The new thought sank like a rock in his belly as louder sirens reached his ears.

Letting emotion distract him again. He glanced at Valena. "We need to leave before the police get here."

Valena rose to her feet, still holding Savannah. "Let's go."

Something stronger than he'd ever felt gripped his heart at the sight she made—so brave, so beautiful despite everything they'd been through. And trust still shone in her eyes.

He prayed he wouldn't let her down.

▭

Valena smoothed Sammy's silky hair, relieved he'd gone back to sleep in the taxi after waking briefly. Savannah was also finally calm, sleeping in her car seat on the other side of Valena, her little features relaxed and peaceful.

Valena wished she could borrow some of that peace herself to calm her still-tense muscles. They'd had to sneak out of the hotel through the emergency exit as if they were the criminals. And catching a taxi at three a.m. when they had two kids in car seats hadn't been easy. But somehow she didn't mind much.

Cooper had kept them safe from harm again. And he'd dried Savannah's tears.

Valena had to fight to hold back tears of her own when he had done that. She'd been wrong. Very wrong. Cooper was nothing like her dad. She never thought she'd meet a man who was actually suited to being a husband and father. Someone she felt she could raise a family with.

Part of her insisted he was too good to be true. That part of her was quick to remind her of his adventurous streak, his love of danger. But his work wasn't actually dangerous. Not usually. He probably mostly handled installing security systems like he had for Lance.

He wasn't a career military man like her dad. He wasn't married to the government, committed to keeping its secrets and telling its lies, willing to give the government precedence over family. She could live with the securities stuff.

She looked at him, sitting in the front passenger seat next to the driver.

Even from that distance he seemed to exude confidence and strength. Like everything would be all right because he would keep them safe.

As if he sensed her gaze, he turned his head, his eyes filled with that blend of concern and caring she could get used to. "Are you okay?"

She nodded, a strange smile settling on her lips. She shouldn't be happy under these circumstances. A drug cartel had just tried to kill them. But somehow the future was looking brighter than she'd ever dreamed.

A murmur from Sammy drew her gaze.

The driver slammed on the brakes.

Valena threw her arms in front of the twins as the taxi screeched to a halt.

She peered through the windshield

A black SUV stood in their path, parked lengthwise across the dark street. The cartel?

Her gaze jumped to Cooper. Fell on an empty seat.

He wasn't there. Where had he gone? His door was slightly open.

A knock on the driver's window made her start.

The driver said something in Spanish, his voice shaky as he lowered the window.

Agent Hinds held up his ID.

Not cartel. Her heart rate slowed slightly, even as Hinds' cold smile sent a shiver through her.

Another agent caught her eye as he moved up to the front passenger door and looked in where Cooper had been.

"I'll have to take your passengers and move them to another vehicle." Hinds pinned the poor driver with a hard look that didn't seem necessary.

The driver's wide eyes and panicked glances at the agents suggested he'd sooner have a heart attack than try to stop them.

The agent on the passenger side opened the back door at the same time Hinds opened the door on the other side.

The extra gun was out of her reach in the backpack on the floor. She couldn't risk making a move with the twins on either side of her.

"I see White already abandoned you." Hinds bent to look at Valena. "Or did you leave him after the unfortunate shooting spree at the hotel? So much for the extraordinary abilities of Cooper White."

Valena barely held back the urge to whack the smirk off his face. But where had Cooper gone? He couldn't have left them.

"Time to join the good side." Hinds reached for Sammy's car seat.

"I'll get him." Valena's glare delivered as much of a threat as her sharp tone. He better not miss it. And whatever Cooper was planning, he had better do it soon.

Hinds didn't move as he assessed her. "We don't have time for delay." He leaned in to unclip the straps on Sammy.

"Hold it."

Her heart leaped at the sound of Cooper's voice behind Hinds.

His arm snaked around the agent's neck.

Hinds' smirk returned. "You know I can get out of this hold."

"If I recall from our training matches, you can't get out of mine. And I've got a weapon in your back this time without a regulation not to use it."

The smile dropped.

"Tell your other agents to back off and return to their vehicles."

Hinds nodded, looking across the car. "Do it."

The extra agent backed away. A few others she hadn't noticed standing at a distance followed him to the SUV and a car she could see peeking out from behind the larger vehicle.

"Now hand your weapon to Valena, butt first."

Hinds slowly removed his gun from the holster under his jacket and extended it to her, Cooper watching the exchange over his shoulder. "What are you going to do with all that money, White?"

"What money?" Cooper's confident gaze went to Valena, reassuring her he had the situation under control.

"The drug money you're trying to take. I know what you and Acker are up to."

"Hinds, as usual, you don't have a clue what's really going on. And I can see you're just as good a judge of character as ever." A wry smile angled Cooper's lips. "Unfortunately, I don't have time to fill you in because we're far too busy doing what you should be doing."

Cooper released his hold on Hinds' neck and backed up, still pointing his Glock at the agent. "Now join your buddies and don't try anything. You've seen me shoot."

Hinds walked past the taxi and rounded it to head for the SUV. He paused, but didn't look back. "We're not done, White."

"Keep moving."

Hinds obeyed as Cooper followed his progress with a steady glare.

"Close the door." Cooper didn't look at Valena while she did as he said, and he walked around the rear of the taxi, shutting the opposite back door without taking his eyes and gun off the retreating agent.

He slipped into the front seat and glanced at the driver. "Go."

The driver didn't move, saying something in Spanish.

Cooper spewed a response in rapid Spanish, holding up the gun.

The driver hit the gas.

But Valena and her churning stomach had the feeling they hadn't seen the last of Agent Hinds.

CHAPTER
TWENTY-THREE

COOPER WATCHED as the rising sun cast soft light on the twins, playing on the playground of another twenty-four-hour fast-food restaurant.

Valena's musical chuckle drew his gaze to her across the table. The sunlight touched her cheeks and made her violet eyes glitter. "I hadn't set foot in a fast-food restaurant for ten years. Now I've been in two in the last two days."

But she was smiling about it. A smile he could easily stay lost in for hours. A pleasant change from fighting him at every step as she had at first. She'd proven to be a real trooper. Actually, she'd turned out to be a valuable partner in this.

Partner. The word his mind grabbed gave him pause. Would she be a good life partner, too? She was fiercely devoted to those she loved, she cared deeply, she was protective, coura-geous…beautiful.

"I have to admit your handling of Hinds was impressive. I didn't mind seeing that smirk finally get wiped off his face." The twinkle in her eyes made his heart skip a beat.

He mentally added a great sense of humor to the list, too. "Glad I could finally impress you." *What?* Now he was flirting with her. He had to knock it off. The last time he'd let himself get distracted, bullets flew through the window.

He sobered as he scanned the parking lot through the windows and checked the rest of the restaurant, only a few unsuspicious customers eating at tables and ordering at the counter. "I'm afraid the smirk isn't permanently gone. That was too easy."

Her eyebrows lifted. "I thought you schooled Hinds pretty thoroughly."

He shook his head, checking on the twins who climbed up the short slide. "Sure, I was better than Hinds at some things, but he's still a fighter. No DEA agent would have given up that easily. I left him more than one chance to try something."

"You mean like when you had him hand me his gun."

Smart, too. The list of her positive traits was growing. And he shouldn't be thinking about it. "Exactly."

"Do you think Hinds is the mole, and he didn't want to do anything to interfere with the cartel's plans?"

"Could be. But as much as I don't see eye-to-eye with Hinds, I have a hard time picturing him as a traitor to his country."

She held his gaze. "Not everyone is like you, Cooper."

His pulse took off in a sprint at the look in her eyes. Could that be respect? And something softer? He swallowed. "I'm not perfect."

She laughed, that lilting sound that did odd things to his heart. "You had the intelligence to leave the DEA."

For some reason the comment stung, but he knew from her smile she didn't mean any harm.

"Truthfully, I can't imagine you ever having been one of them. All the lies and secrets. Always running around to do the government's bidding." She leaned forward over the table between them, cupping her elbows in her hands. "Why did you ever sign up for that?"

He shrugged, an uncomfortable sensation he didn't quite understand stirring in his belly. "Some of my buddies from SF got mixed up with drugs, trying to handle what we'd encountered over there. I saw firsthand what addiction does." Dark memories flashed through his mind, launching the old familiar feeling of righteous anger and drive that used to fuel his days with the DEA. "I couldn't rest in some cushy office job while an enemy like that ravaged my country."

Valena's smile faded as she watched him. "That's very noble. But at least you didn't have a family you abandoned to do that."

His gut twisted at the sadness in her eyes. "I'm sure your dad didn't mean to do that." Cooper took a breath, trying to choose his words carefully. "Maybe he wanted to protect you from the danger he saw could come home if he didn't stop it."

She shifted her gaze to the children who giggled as they chatted with each other. "You're right. He would've died to protect us." She turned back to Cooper, her eyes darkened to purple. "But he didn't want to live with us."

There they were. Back to her pain and his inability to help her. But, oh, how his heart ached to do something. He covered her hand with his on the table. "I'm so sorry."

She turned her hand over, grasping his from underneath and sending fire pulsing through his veins. "And I'm sorry for what you must have gone through in the Army...at the DEA. I know that's a hard life. I'm glad it's over for you."

He nodded, her words cooling the fire until it lodged in his vessels like a block of ice.

Adrenaline pushed Cooper faster as he easily picked the lock and opened the front door of Carissa Wulford's house. He walked inside with the calm stride of an expected house guest.

Closing the door behind him, he launched into action, hurrying across black marble tiles to the hallway. He quickly found the second door, which was closed. He hadn't seen anyone enter in the last hour since he and Valena had watched Wulford leave for work, so the office should be empty.

He still turned the knob quietly, letting the door swing all the way open so he could see the whole room.

The modern office was sparsely decorated with a sleek silver and black desk, cabinets along the wall and some weird art pieces. No cameras hung from the ceiling.

A massive computer monitor sat on the glass-topped desk.

He went for the computer and sat in the black swivel chair in front of it.

Shifting the mouse to light up the monitor, he started to install the detection software. With a computer this new, he should be out in five minutes or less.

His phone buzzed in his jacket pocket.

He pulled it out.

A text from Valena's new phone. *Someone's coming to the door.*

"EXCUSE ME." Valena forced a friendly smile as the older woman turned back from the front door.

An answering smile brightened the woman's face as she looked at Savannah in Valena's arms and Sammy, climbing up the steps while holding Valena's hand. "Well, who do we have here?"

Valena held back a sigh of relief that the woman seemed to love children. "Sammy and Savannah."

"Aww." The woman's salt and pepper bangs blew in the gentle breeze as she stepped toward Sammy. "Aren't you both beautiful?" Her gaze lifted to rest on Savannah. "Are you two twins?"

"Tins." Savannah held up one finger.

The woman laughed and Valena joined in, hoping to override the pounding of her heart.

Was Cooper done yet?

"So what brings you here with your little ones?" Friendly blue eyes waited for Valena's answer.

"Is Carissa Wulford at home, do you know?"

The pattern of faint lines crossing the woman's brow deepened. "No, she'd be gone to work right now. Did you need to see her?"

"Well..." Valena bit her lip as if trying to make a decision. Cooper had better be leaving the house by now because she was running out of ideas. "I guess we can wait. We've been traveling a long time to get here, but..." At least that was true. She refused to let all this adventure stuff turn her into someone who lied to get what she wanted.

"I'd love to invite you inside to wait, but I really shouldn't. Ms. Wulford is very security conscious." The woman's small mouth pulled into a frown.

"Oh, I know. Security is always a big deal to Carissa." Valena breathed a laugh and smiled, probably too broadly. "It's fine. We'll just go get some breakfast and come back later."

"Do you have her cell phone number?" Her thinning eyebrows pulled together.

"Oh, yes, of course." Valena started to turn Sammy back toward the stairs. Cooper had probably already left by the back door. Hopefully. "She doesn't check her messages very often sometimes."

"Well, maybe try her again."

Valena smiled and nodded over her shoulder as she guided Sammy down the stairs. "Thank you for your help."

"You're welcome. Take care of those adorable children." She waved as they reached the sidewalk.

"Thank you. I will." Valena smiled as Savannah and Sammy returned the wave. Valena looked down at Sammy. "Let's go back to the car now." She casually glanced around as she walked in the direction of their rented car, parked two large houses up the curved street. Keeping her gaze moving, she tried to subtly check the portion of the yard and house that she could see.

No Cooper.

Her stomach clenched. Had he made it out? Did she need to go back?

"Cooper." Sammy pointed ahead, a big smile on his face.

Her heart lurched at the sight of Cooper, leaning against the gray car. She held back the silly grin that wanted to reach her face as they neared. "When did Sammy learn to say your name?"

Cooper straightened, the corner of his mouth tucking. "He's a smart kid. Aren't you, buddy?" He ducked and rushed at Sammy with a grin, eliciting a squeal as he swept the boy into the air. He settled Sammy on one arm and opened the back door for Valena.

She paused at the door and met his twinkling gaze. "Did you get it?"

His mouth straightened as he nodded. "It's all set up. Now all we have to do is watch and wait."

Anxiety and impatience curdled in her belly. If only the danger could all be over now.

He cupped her elbow with his fingers. "This will work. I promise."

She looked into those dark eyes. Nothing she'd ever wanted so badly had worked out. Maybe, with Cooper, things could be different this time.

But a shadow lurked in her mind, as if disaster was waiting, just around the corner.

———

"This is it." Cooper leaned into the screen of the notebook computer as Valena came to stand beside his chair at the dining table.

Her warmth next to him only sped his pulse more as he watched Carissa Wulford begin to use her home computer.

The two recordings showed up on his screen simultaneously—the video of her, sitting in front of her own computer and the recording of her screen, which let him see every move she made while using the computer.

Father, please let this work.

The webcam recording was set to catch sound, but she worked silently, and no noise interrupted the hush in the two-bedroom apartment they'd rented for the night.

He hadn't seen the kids for a while. "Are the twins asleep?"

Valena nodded, her arm brushing his shoulder as she leaned to look closer. "Is she accessing the bank database?"

"Looks like it."

Wulford rapidly typed in a username and password.

"I'm betting *Sarah Olson* isn't her username, huh?" Wry humor colored Valena's tone.

"Good guess."

Wulford opened bank records, then moved on to accessing individual accounts. She opened one that Lance's flash drive had included, then another one.

"Those are the accounts the drug money went into."

"Yep. Here we go." His breathing shallowed as he watched Wulford transfer the deposits, consistent with the days and times Lance had documented, from those accounts to others. Then she logged out of the system and logged back in as another user. She transferred the money from the accounts she'd just deposited it in and transferred the loot again, dividing it into multiple accounts.

"Whoa." Valena's mouth gaped when Wulford doctored the times and dates of the transfers to appear as if they'd been done on separate business days.

Wulford used yet another username to make her final move. She transferred the funds from the seven accounts to one offshore account, again adjusting the time and date records of the transactions to make them appear normal.

Valena turned her head to Cooper, still leaning over as her beautiful violet eyes widened.

He grinned. "Got her."

A smile curved Valena's lips, making Cooper's heart jump against his ribs.

"Finally." A woman's voice drew their gazes back to the screen. Wulford had an email open. Something that had prompted her remark.

Cooper's gaze hit the text on the screen.

Wizard finished. No need for doubles. Back to business as usual.

Horror gripped him from the inside out.

"What does that mean?"

He couldn't answer, not with the pain searing through his heart.

"Cooper?" Valena touched his shoulder, her hand seeping warmth through his sweater, giving him the strength to meet her gaze.

He swallowed. "Lance is dead."

CHAPTER
TWENTY-FIVE

COOPER PUSHED off the bed and paced to one of the windows, giving up on sleep. Standing to the side, he pulled the closed blinds a quarter inch away from the wall and peered across the darkness to the empty parking lot opposite the upper-level apartment.

But he didn't have to watch for shooters or kidnappers any longer. His heart plummeted to his stomach as the new reality slammed into him. It was good the cartel didn't want the twins now. But he'd give his life to have them stop for a different reason.

If only he had moved faster on this case. If he'd closed in on the auditor more quickly, he could have gotten the evidence to the right people fast enough that Lance…

Cooper raked a hand through his hair, reining in the urge to punch the wall.

Why hadn't Lance kept him up to speed on this case all along? He could've kept him in the loop, and Cooper could have already been helping him nail the cartel before any of this had happened.

Just like when they were both DEA.

The truth lodged like a rock in his gut.

If he had never left the agency, this wouldn't have happened. He could have saved Lance's life if he'd still been there. With Cooper to trust, Lance wouldn't have had to work alone. Cooper could have helped him find the snitch and bring down the cartel.

Cooper clenched his fists as he stalked back to the bed. Why had he ever left the DEA in the first place?

Gillian. She hadn't wanted him to be gone so much, like when he was an internationally posted agent. She said he'd have to be around more if he wanted to marry her, if he was really committed.

He'd done it for her. Just like he'd stopped going to his church because she hadn't liked it. Then that had turned into not going to church at all because she never found one she liked.

Cooper sank to the edge of the bedspread.

But God had seemed so distant that whole time. Like now. He used to feel so close, so present in Cooper's life. What had happened?

Jesus Christ is the same yesterday and today and forever. The Bible verse he had memorized long ago came to his mind. Jesus never changed. And didn't He promise never to leave, too? Cooper searched the files of his memory for the verse. *I will never leave you nor forsake you.*

God hadn't left Cooper. He hadn't pulled away. Cooper had.

Probably starting with Gillian. His parents had warned him. They didn't think she was a Christian. But he was in love. He'd believed that every glimpse of kindness and goodness in her meant she was a believer.

She'd gone along with the church thing at first, but then she'd started to invent excuses not to go. And somehow, it had ended with him not going either. He'd eventually given up reading the Bible and praying because both only made him feel guilty. He hadn't even prayed about quitting the DEA, the work he had once felt so strongly the Lord had called him to do.

Was he about to make the same mistake again? He couldn't deny the growing feelings he had for Valena. But she wasn't a Christian. He wouldn't lie to himself about that again. And she'd made her dislike of government jobs very clear.

Cooper took a deep breath and slid off the bed, dropping to his knees on the floor. For the first time in a very long time, he knew he needed to find out what God wanted him to do.

As soon as Cooper began to pray, a wave of peace brought the truth to his soul—God wasn't far away at all. He was right there with open arms, waiting for His child to come home.

▭

"I'm sorry we have to move the twins again."

Valena paused midway through folding Savannah's pajama top and looked at Cooper.

"I know it's not good for them." His eyebrows drew together in the heavy expression he'd worn all morning. The sadness in his eyes mirrored the grief that squeezed her own heart.

"At least the cartel won't be chasing us anymore." She set the top aside and grabbed the pajama pants. "And I had time to do laundry." She held up the little pants, forcing a weak smile. "I'm glad you found this place. Two bedrooms and a washer and dryer is pure luxury these days."

His attempt at a return smile felt even more pitiful than hers. "I wish I could take you all home right away, but we have to turn in this evidence before anyone finds out we have it. Before the cartel can try to cover its tracks. Saul is a terrific prosecutor—once we get him the evidence, he'll be able to get the warrants and arrests made before the DEA snitch can open his mouth."

"Or hers." Valena raised her eyebrows, accompanied by a teasing smile.

Cooper chuckled, a sound that trickled down her spine to her toes. "Sorry. I forgot equal opportunity in everything, even criminal activity."

At least she finally got him to lose the dark expression for a moment. Though the pain hadn't left her heart any more than it had probably left his. And it wouldn't for a long time.

She stuffed the rest of the clean clothes into the backpack and turned to look at Sammy and Savannah, sitting on the floor with the iPad as Savannah told Sammy one of her somewhat unintelligible stories.

Someday, too soon, Valena would have to tell them the device was from their dad. That it was all he'd left them. She'd have to tell them who their dad was. What would she say? A man who'd chosen the government and adventure over his children?

"Our favorite auditor is back." Cooper stood by the computer that sat on the dining table, the screen tilted so he could see from his standing position.

Valena walked to his side, her heart rate rising as she stopped close to him. She forced her attention from him to the computer, a voice coming from the speakers.

"I don't know." Carissa Wulford sat in front of the webcam, her hair pushed back behind a Bluetooth earpiece hooked on her ear. "My housekeeper just told me a woman was at my house yesterday, looking for me. She said the woman didn't come in, but she had two kids with her."

Valena's throat shrank as her breathing shallowed.

"A boy and a girl. Twins."

Her heart stopped.

Cooper touched her elbow, his hand like a steady anchor in the fear that washed over her.

"They may have tried to look at my files or change them somehow." Carissa stared hard at her screen while Cooper's other video image showed she was checking her documents, banking files, and financial forms. "How can I tell if they've done anything on my computer?" She pressed her lips together. "What?" Her gaze shifted away like she was listening to the person on the other end. "You think they might have—"

She closed her mouth and clicked through to areas Valena didn't quite follow. But she recognized the name of the spying software Cooper had installed as it came up on the screen.

Carissa stood, leaving the view of the camera.

The screen went black.

"Let's go." Cooper's voice was a deep growl as he slammed the computer shut and stuffed it in the backpack on the table.

"What just happened?" The feeling in the pit of her stomach gave her the answer that it wasn't good.

"She pulled the plug on the computer." He went to the twins, reaching for Sammy.

Sammy smiled and turned into Cooper's chest as he picked the boy up.

"They know what we've done, what we've got." He returned to the table and lifted the backpack, slinging the strap over his shoulder.

"But maybe she won't fig—"

"All she has to do is think back to what she did on her computer yesterday after we were there." His gaze held an edge as he looked at Valena over Sammy's head. "It will only take her a few minutes, if that."

"But why does it matter? You said your Army buddy, Saul, will be able to get her with the evidence we have. So what can they do?"

"You're right, we have solid evidence. She shouldn't be

able to get out of it easily. But right now, all that matters is we have to leave as quickly as possible." He bent to grab Sammy's car seat from the floor.

Valena's heart sprinted at his sudden urgency. "What are you not telling me?"

He stopped and met her gaze. "The cartel has too much at stake here. We've gone for the jugular."

She looked at him, willing him not to mean what she thought he did.

His eyes softened slightly, but his tone was no less grim when he finished. "Now that they know what we've got, they'll probably do two things. Kill Wulford. And kill us."

TWENTY-SIX

COOPER SET the wipers to a higher setting, but the old car they'd bought off the lawn of an elderly junk collector apparently needed new blades, among many other repairs.

Snow blew into the windshield in gusts, sometimes forming a curtain of white he could barely see through. Plows hadn't had a chance to catch up with the blizzard that had begun as a light flurry before rapidly increasing to a deluge.

They were apparently driving into the storm as they traveled east, since the snow on the roads became thicker and the accumulation in ditches looked deeper the farther they drove. At least the twins slept through it all, blissfully unaware of danger or the growing tension he sensed from Valena as she sat silently in the passenger seat beside him.

"We should stop."

He glanced at her. "We can't stop. We don't know how close the cartel is."

"If you just pull over for a little bit, we can wait out the worst of this." She stared out the windshield at the blizzard conditions. "It isn't safe to drive in."

"It's not safe to stop either. We have to beat the cartel to

Washington and hand the evidence over to Saul. Then we can stop."

"We shouldn't give your friend the evidence either. I won't risk the twins' lives. You said the cartel wants to kill them now." Her eyes flashed in the dimming light as the blizzard and dusk robbed the sky of the sun.

"They'll want to kill us because of what we know, what we have. If the kids are with us..." The tires lost traction on the slippery road. He took his foot off the gas, keeping the wheel straight as the car righted itself. This time.

"We should let the DEA finish this. We can give them the evidence we have now and let them handle it."

Cooper sent her a disbelieving stare. "Are you kidding me? There's a mole in the DEA. Whoever it is could destroy the evidence before it sees the light of a courtroom."

"You said you don't think Hinds is the mole. We can give it to him. He's probably somewhere close, following us."

Cooper tightened his grip on the wheel, trying to see through the blustering snow. "There's no way I'm letting Hinds finish Lance's work. He doesn't deserve the credit this will bring."

Silence. Cooper finally looked at her to see why she was so quiet.

An unreadable stare met his gaze. "So that's it. You want the credit, don't you? You think the DEA will take you back if you can take down a drug cartel."

He looked at the road and swallowed. "I'm sure they will."

"You didn't say you wanted to go back." Disappointment clutched her voice.

"You didn't want me to say it."

"That's not fair. I thought we were being honest with each other. I thought..."

He glanced over, catching the pain in her eyes before she looked away.

"I thought we might have a future. Together."

His chest felt like someone was pinching it in a vise. But he still had to tell her the truth. "We couldn't, Valena. I can't...be with you because we don't share the same faith. You're not a Christian."

"Don't give me that." Her eyes sparked as she swung her head to glare at him. "I don't believe that excuse for a second. This is about the job. You're picking the DEA over me." She let out a humorless laugh and looked out the window again. "I was right. You really are just like my dad. I suppose it's a good thing this came up now before we had something to regret."

Her shots hit their target, making anger rise to cover his wounds. He opened his mouth to defend himself, but she spoke first.

"I would've ended up like my mother. Alone in a church, lighting candles for the rest of my life."

The image and the hurt that lined Valena's voice beneath her fury doused his urge to return fire. "This isn't about the job, Valena." He looked at her, hoping she'd turn to see the sincerity in his eyes. "It's about God. It's about finally doing what He wants me to do after too many years of trying to do everything my own way."

She still stared out the window.

"You said some things shouldn't be sacrificed, and you're right."

That brought her gaze to his face.

"The one thing I never should have sacrificed was my relationship with Jesus, living my life to please Him." Cooper watched the road, the snow growing deeper. "I'm still figuring out again what that looks like, but I know part of it is following God's call for my life." He threw her a glance. "And part of it is obeying His command that I not be attached to someone who isn't a follower of Jesus."

"So you're going to clean up your life? Follow the rules?"

Cynicism nearly dripped from her tone. "Never helped my mom."

"But it isn't about following the rules and trying to win God's favor. God doesn't need good behavior or candle-lighting to please Him or to get Him to do things. He isn't like a gum machine—put in good behavior and get out what you want."

Valena stared through the windshield, her jaw working like she was clenching her teeth.

Father, please let her hear me. His breath caught with a kind of desperation he'd never felt before. "God offers salvation to anyone who asks, anyone who believes that Jesus died to save them from their sins. Anyone who is ready to love and trust Him. Nobody can earn God's salvation. All you can do is ask for it and accept it as a free gift."

Her silence pulled his gaze to her for as long as he could risk ignoring the road.

But she'd turned her head completely away. "Do you know how many times I asked God for help as a kid?" Her voice was raw, like an open wound he didn't dare touch. "I begged Him for it on the worst night of my life, just for Him to bring my dad home." She kept her face toward the side window, but Cooper could feel her pain as if it were his own. "That shouldn't have been too much to ask. But He didn't do it. He didn't save me at all."

Father, give me the right words. The lesson He had just taught Cooper seemed like the best place to start. "God always comes to the rescue, but it's not always the way we expect. I just learned that the hard way. God doesn't leave us, we leave Him."

"That's ridiculous."

Not the response he'd hoped for. Cooper gripped the wheel as the tires skidded.

"God's never been anything but missing from my life."

The tires gripped again, and Cooper glanced at Valena. "God already came to your rescue in a more important way when he sent His Son Jesus to die on the cross for your sins."

"I know the story."

"Then you should also know that He died to save you from something even worse than your childhood."

"From hell?" Her tone carried the smirk without him having to see it.

"Yes, from eternity without your heavenly Father, Who's the perfect, loving Father you've always wanted. The One Who promises to never leave you nor forsake you." The reminder, so fresh in his own heart, sent warmth from his soul through his body. He knew he had to tell her the rest of the truth. "I know you won't believe this right now, Valena, but I care about you, too."

Her gaze jerked back to him.

"As much as I'd like to pursue a relationship with you, that doesn't matter at all compared to the importance of you having the right relationship with Christ. Whatever happens, I hope you'll—"

Headlights appeared out of the white cloud. In their lane.

"Cooper!"

"Hold on!" He swung the car out of the truck's path, but the tires lost traction.

The car careened out of control, spun into a turn, then another.

A forest of black trees waited for them as they spiraled toward the edge of the road.

On Valena's side.

He yanked the wheel, thrusting the car into one more spin that gave him the view of the rapidly approaching line of trees.

Valena screamed.

Jesus, please. The children.

A crushing impact wrenched his body.

TWENTY-SEVEN

BREATH RUSHED into Valena's lungs. Her brain pushed through sludge to process what had just happened in the span of a few seconds.

The twins.

She looked into the back seat.

Sammy and Savannah both cried, but their car seats were still strapped in place, the children both in them where they should be. They didn't look hurt. No blood that she could see.

"It's okay. You're okay." She twisted around. "Cooper?"

His head hung forward, almost touching the steering wheel.

"Cooper?" Her gaze fell to the broken glass that covered his jeans. Along with blood.

Her heart seized.

She unbuckled her seatbelt and leaned toward him to try to see his face.

A drop of blood fell from the left side of his head. She couldn't see how bad a gash or cut he might have.

A thick tree limb stuck through the window, protruding about five inches inside the car with red splattered on its brown and green bark. Cooper's head must have been struck by the branch.

"Cooper? Can you hear me?" What if he was dying? Or already—

Her throat closed, nearly halting her oxygen. He couldn't be.

She started to move closer to him, but stopped when glass pricked her hand.

The middle seat between them was covered in broken shards.

She pulled her jacket sleeve out over her hand and used the fabric to swipe the pieces onto the floor. Scooting to him over the seat, she reached to check for a pulse on his neck.

His skin was warm. A small beat thumped against her fingers.

Her own heart beat again in response.

"Don't move."

She froze at the sound of the male voice outside Cooper's window.

"There's an agent behind you, too."

Hinds? She risked tilting her head to see behind Cooper.

The agent she'd hoped never to see again watched her with his cool green eyes. And a gun.

"Cooper's hurt."

"So I see. Where's his weapon?"

"You don't understand. He needs help. I don't know how badly he's injured."

"Where is his weapon?"

"In his holster! You need to call 911."

"Get out of the car, and we'll take care of him."

She turned to her door, glaring at the other agent who stood there, also with his gun raised. She shoved the door open and stepped into the snow, sinking a foot into the deep drift.

Snow tumbled into the tops of her boots, but she ignored the freezing sensation as it found its way to her skin between her jeans and socks.

Hinds rounded the back of the car to her side, his gun returned to his holster. "Get the kids. You're coming with us."

"In your dreams."

He smiled, that horrible smirk only Cooper seemed to be able to wipe off. "The longer you take, the longer it will be before White gets help. I won't call for paramedics until you're in the SUV."

"You're kidding."

"I don't kid about capturing a money launderer."

"You mean Cooper?"

"Get the children."

The guy was a creep, No wonder Cooper didn't like him. Cooper hadn't wanted her to go with the DEA, but wouldn't he feel differently if he knew his life was on the line?

And two agents were there with guns, probably more with the two SUVs and the car that she glimpsed through the falling snow, parked alongside the road. She didn't really have any choice but to cooperate. Or feign cooperation until she saw a chance to escape with the twins.

At least the DEA had found them instead of the cartel. She had some connections through her dad—she could fight the DEA if they tried to take the children. But they wouldn't hurt the twins. Not physically. At the moment, that was the most important thing.

She opened the back door and reached in to unstrap Savannah from her car seat.

"Careful."

She paused at Hinds' warning.

"I know you have an extra weapon. Where is it?"

"In the glove compartment." Hinds' gun was there. The

deputy's was in the backpack on the floor, but Hinds didn't need to know that.

"Just keep your hands on the kid where I can see them. Play nice, and I'll make sure White gets the help he needs."

Anger simmered in her stomach. Hard to believe Hinds was supposed to be one of the good guys.

She lifted Savannah from the seat, her heart twisting at the sight of the tears on her little angel's face.

Savannah sobbed and buried her head against Valena's neck.

An agent already had Sammy out of the car by the time she made it to his side.

She reached to take him, and the stocky agent handed him over without protest. Probably glad not to have to handle any children.

She trudged through the deep snow up the slope to the road, cold flakes wetting her cheeks and clinging to her eyelashes.

Her heart squeezed. She didn't know which was worse, heading for the vehicle of agents who might try to take the twins from her or leaving Cooper behind, injured and alone with his enemies.

A blond-haired agent opened the door of the SUV as she neared.

She stepped onto the low floor and sat on the bench seat with the children, Savannah still clinging to her and Sammy taking in everything with his big eyes.

Hinds appeared by the open door, the white world back-lighting him in an appropriately dark shadow. He held up his phone. "I've put in a call. White will receive all the help he needs."

"He shouldn't be alone. He could—"

"I'm leaving agents here with him. Believe me, I'm not about to let him get away."

Of course. Hinds still thought Cooper was a criminal.

"We need the car seats for the—"

He slammed the door in her face, plummeting them into semi-darkness. The tinted windows and gray lighting outside made the interior of the SUV feel like a cave. Or a closet.

She pushed back the fear that clawed at her mind as Hinds and the blond-haired agent got into the front, Hinds taking the passenger seat.

The driver pulled onto the snow-covered road, the visibility not much improved since Cooper had been driving.

She looked back as they drove away from the scene.

The old car lodged in the snow at an angle by the trees, Cooper inside.

What if it took too long for the ambulance to reach him in this blizzard? Helplessness tied her stomach in a knot. She'd pray if she didn't already know it wouldn't do any good.

"Don't worry about White."

She shifted forward to see Hinds' smirk as he rotated toward her.

"We'll take care of him. And when he wakes up and finds out we have you and the children, I'm sure he'll be much more cooperative, too."

She stroked Savannah's curls, trying to focus on the little girl's dissipating crying rather than the urge to ring the agent's neck.

"You know, this couldn't have gone better than if I'd planned it myself. Which I did, partially, of course." Hinds turned to face the front, apparently content to hear his own voice without her reactions. "Frankly, I'm not sure Lance would have ever been lured to us by holding his children. But Cooper was always a soft touch. He'll talk to guarantee a good future for the children."

Hinds shot Valena a twisty grin. "From what I've seen, he has a special reason to want to help you."

Heat surged to her cheeks—from anger rather than the embarrassment Hinds probably hoped for. Had he seen them in the hotel? When Cooper gave her the almost-kiss? Typical government ploy to be watching and controlling. He wouldn't get the satisfaction of a reaction from her.

"We've had you in sight for some time. I decided it would be easier to sit back and watch what you were up to. Easier to let the mouse lead us to the cheese. I figured White would eventually take us directly to Acker. Or to whatever they were planning to do."

The man was so smug and superior, he had to be the mole. She had more than a few things to say to him. "I suppose you're responsible for Lance needing to go off the grid, too?" Fury laced her tone. "For the twins being in danger? I suppose you enjoy putting children's lives on the line just to solve a case?"

"What are you talking about?" For once, the smirk was nowhere in sight as he looked back at her.

"The mole in the DEA."

His thin lips formed a slash. "Did White tell you there was a leak in the DEA?"

"It's obvious, isn't it?"

"Only if you've been conned by—"

A pop pierced the air, and blood splattered the windshield.

The twins screamed.

Valena instinctively clutched them close, turning their heads into her chest, away from anything they might see.

Her brain seemed to detach from her emotions and her body.

Hinds' hand fell limp by the seat, as if in slow motion.

The driver said something. At least his mouth moved. He waved a gun. Kept driving.

The cool fog of her brain started to clear, allowed her to hear her pulse thundering in her ears, the agent behind the wheel yelling for her to shut the children up and not make a move.

She'd found the mole.

And he was taking them to the cartel.

<hr>

"Cooper?" Valena's voice reached for him in the darkness.

Valena. The children.

A faint sense of alarm pushed Cooper to force his heavy lids open.

Light hit his pupil, and a surge of pain shot through his head.

The jolt dissipated, but a pounding in his head remained, like a giant was hitting it with a sledge hammer. His whole body ached. Fiery pain flamed in his shoulder. His hip, too. Why—

They'd crashed.

He jerked his head to see Valena, paying for the movement with another shot of pain.

Her seat was empty.

"Take it easy, man."

He turned to the voice on his left.

Agent Baker watched him next to a branch that stabbed the air in front of Cooper's face. So the DEA had found them.

"Where's Valena? The twins?"

"They're safe."

"Where?"

"Hinds has them."

Terrific. He had split them up as soon as he could. And now he'd try to sell more lies to Valena. Would she believe him?

"Where did he take them?" Cooper fumbled through

broken glass to unbuckle his seat belt, noting the blood spatters and tiny cuts on his hand.

"Back to Chicago. They're flying out of O'Hare."

Cooper started to slide to the passenger side since the driver's door was crunched beyond use.

Pain slammed into him like a tank. He stopped. Hadn't felt this bad since that IED had gone off too close to him during his first deployment.

"You shouldn't be moving. You need medical attention." Baker's voice drifted, probably making his way around the car.

As if Cooper would sit still when Valena and the twins needed him. He gritted his aching teeth and continued to slide to the passenger door.

He pushed it open, but Baker grabbed the door, blocking his way.

"I'm fine." Thank the Lord it was Baker and not some other agent he didn't know. He met his former co-worker's gaze. "You know Hinds. This is going to be hard on them. I need to be there."

He glanced away. "My orders are to keep you here until you get medical attention, then bring you in separately."

Cooper got to his feet in the small space Baker left him behind the door, summoning all the strength he had not to wince at the pain. He held eye contact with the agent. "You know me, Baker. And you know Lance. Do you really think we've turned on the DEA and everything it stands for?"

The shift of color in Baker's blue eyes was Cooper's answer.

"Let me prove it."

Baker released his hold on the door and backed off, letting out a sigh.

Cooper trudged through the snow, the pain with the first steps robbing him of breath.

Baker grabbed Cooper's arm and slung it over his neck.

Cooper bit back a cry at the surge in his injured shoulder and leaned on Baker, forcing himself to accept the help and get to the waiting SUV that much faster.

To Valena and the twins.

"You're picking the DEA over me."

The memory of Valena's face pushed even his pain to the background. Her beautiful eyes had looked at him with such hurt. Betrayal. She'd looked so...alone.

Please, Father, keep them safe. Please be with them when I can't. Cooper let go of Baker as soon as they reached the SUV, his strength returning as the pain became more bearable.

He hauled himself up onto the front seat, picturing Valena and the twins with Hinds. At least the DEA had taken them instead of the cartel. They wouldn't be in physical danger.

Things could be much worse.

CHAPTER
TWENTY-EIGHT

THE MOLE'S eyes stuck to Valena like a leech.

The man who had shot Hinds kept his gun pointed at her from his perch on the edge of the desk in the small office. He'd kept the suppressor on the gun he had used on Hinds, probably to show he was equally ready to shoot her.

As if she would try anything with the other two men in the room, one looking uncomfortable on a rusted chair by the wall and the other leaning against the doorway. Well, she might, but it seemed strange he would expect it.

Then again, his look was more lecherous than threatening.

The twins were stiff and silent in her lap on the metal folding chair, seeming to sense the gravity of the situation and the unfriendliness of their captors.

Tired of racing, her heart rate had settled into a holding pattern that mimicked the thugs. They were waiting for something. Or someone. They were as close-lipped as they were hostile, and she wasn't quite ready to try cozying up to the mole. She'd rather take him down if she could figure out how.

He was smart enough to keep his distance and not relax his gun.

She should probably test the waters a bit. Feel out their intentions. "Can I get some water? For the kids."

A smile curled his lips. "Just sit tight."

If he would let his guard down for a second, she might be able to get to her phone where he'd set it on the desk.

A bang echoed from elsewhere in the building, like a door swinging shut.

From what she'd seen on the way in, they appeared to be at a pallet factory. She'd thought it must be abandoned, at least tonight.

Which meant the visitor must be what they were waiting for.

The two extra thugs moved to stand at attention in the doorway of the office, while the mole watched through the windows that lined three walls of the office.

Valena craned her neck to look.

A woman in heels and a business suit emerged from an aisle lined with stacks of pallets.

Carissa Wulford.

Another man in baggy black clothes like the rest of them followed her, lagging behind her quick steps.

The men in the doorway stepped aside, clearing the way for her to stalk into the office.

She stopped short, glaring at Valena and the twins. "What are they doing here?"

The mole got to his feet, his brow furrowing as he glanced from Valena to Carissa. "Tomas told me to grab 'em whenever I could."

"I know that." Her snap seemed to puncture the stale air in the room as she stalked in front of the mole and spun toward him, turning her back on Valena. "It's bad enough he foolishly insisted I come here like this, but I'm sure he never intended for you to be so stupid as to bring *them* here at the same time. How dare you endanger my reputation like this?"

Her reputation? She was money laundering for a drug cartel. She must mean her fake reputation as Chief Audit Executive.

"It wasn't my idea." The mole lifted his hands out at his side like a little boy making excuses to his mother. A little boy with a gun. "We don't know how to tell if the flash drive is the right one."

Carissa spun on her five-inch heels to clap her hard stare on Valena. "Does she have it?"

"I don't know."

She tossed him a glare over her shoulder.

"He said it was your mess. You gotta deal with it."

Something flickered in the gaze she brought back to Valena. Fear? But she covered it quickly with a question. "Where's the flash drive?"

"What flash drive?" Valena didn't miss a beat, though her heart picked up speed. Which approach should she take? Pretend she didn't know anything? That might be too obvi—

"The flash drive that you were taking to someone to expose me. It holds a video that you illegally obtained of me in my private residence."

"Illegally?" Valena couldn't help the disbelieving laugh that escaped her lips. "You're running drug money for a cartel."

The woman's lipstick-lined mouth curved into a smile as she took a few steps toward Valena, stopping short of fighting range, especially with the twins on her lap.

"My housekeeper was correct." She scanned Savannah and Sammy. "Such adorable children. But sadly," she fingered the diamond bracelet on her wrist, "I loathe children." Her smile dropped as ice hit her blue eyes. "I'll tell Wentworth here to shoot them if you don't hand over the recording."

Valena's blood turned cold at the sincerity in the threat.

Carissa moved toward Wentworth at the desk and placed

her manicured hand on his shoulder. "Or, perhaps, I'll have him do something else to them. Incapacitation?"

Valena's breath caught. Was the woman seriously *that* evil? Or was she bluffing?

Wentworth glanced at Carissa as if even he was startled.

But Valena almost believed Carissa would hurt the children herself if he refused. Valena would hand over the flash drive right now if she could think of a way it wouldn't get them killed. And if she had it. But Cooper had it.

A pain shot through her torso. If he was alive.

She couldn't think about that right now. She had to get the twins out of here alive, no matter what. She met the horrid woman's gaze, forcing confidence into her own. "I don't have what you want. We have enough evidence to put you away for a long time, but we hid the flash drive. You'll need us alive if you hope to find where it is."

Carissa stared at her for several seconds. Then she smiled. "White has it."

"No, we hid it." Valena kept her tone even and strong. But it didn't work.

"You wouldn't have left the area without the evidence." Carissa turned toward Wentworth. "She wouldn't risk endangering the children if she had it here. White must have it. We'll keep the children as bait. He'll come to us if we have them." Her gaze went to the desk, and she picked up Valena's phone. "Especially if we tell him to."

"What about her?" Wentworth was back to watching Valena.

She met his stare with a glare.

"You'll have to get rid of her."

He lifted his gun.

"Not here, you idiot."

Valena's heart pounded as Carissa pushed his gun down with her hand.

"I'm not going to be tied to any murder. We have to make it look like a natural death. We'll put her in there." She pointed to the door of what looked like a safe under the clock on the wall.

Valena's heart jumped into her throat. Was the woman serious?

"That'll look natural?" Wentworth's skeptical question barely reached Valena's hearing past the blood rushing in her ears.

"Once she suffocates, one of you can bury her out in the snow. It will look like she's a blizzard victim." Carissa glanced at the clock as if she had somewhere more important to be than a murder scene. "Hurry up and get those children away from her."

The two other thugs moved in, reaching for the twins.

"No. You can't take them." Valena wrapped her arms tighter around them, but the men pulled her away, yanking the children from her grasp.

Savannah screeched as the man held her slung over one arm like a ragdoll.

"Ena?" Sammy's mouth crumpled as he reached for her, whimpering when the man who held him gave him a hard shake.

"Stop! Don't hurt them." She couldn't let the children see her fear, imprinting a trauma in their memories they'd never forget. "It's okay, Sammy. Savannah. Ena loves you." She bit back the scream of her heart as she looked at her babies.

A hand jerked her arm painfully.

Wentworth. He pushed her toward the safe.

Her suppressed scream pressed against her lungs as he opened the door. Darkness cloaked the small space, no larger than five feet both ways.

Wentworth reached inside for a light switch, drawing her

gaze to the light fixture in the six-foot-high ceiling of the safe as it turned on.

He lifted his gun and shot. The light fixture shattered, plunging the safe into darkness as her ears rang. Even with a suppressor, the gun was loud enough to pain her ears. "Get in."

Horror nearly choked her. She should fight him. She could kick out his kneecap. But her babies were in the arms of those monsters. They would get hurt before she could save them.

Wentworth shoved her inside.

She spun around, trying to see Savannah and Sammy as he closed the door.

It slammed shut.

Utter darkness met her gaze everywhere she turned.

She released the scream.

"White!" Baker caught up to Cooper as he entered the front of the FBO at O'Hare. "You have to stay with me, or I'm going to cuff you."

"Got it." Cooper slowed to a walk and winced as the pain in his hip and shoulder surged, briefly worse than the constant pounding in his head. "So you're sure the chartered flight was here?"

"Yeah. There's Hal."

A man rose from one of the cushioned chairs in the waiting area. His dark hair had gained silver highlights, but Cooper still recognized the private jet charter pilot from trips through this FBO as an agent.

Hal lowered his bushy eyebrows. "I thought Hinds and Wentworth were my passengers. Along with one more adult and two children."

"They aren't here yet?" Baker glanced at Cooper.

"No." Hal looked at his large wristwatch. "They were supposed to be here an hour ago. Not like Hinds to be late."

That was an understatement. The man lived by a rigid schedule. Had he taken Valena and the twins somewhere else?

"What happened to you?" Hal stared at the side of Cooper's head, where he'd slapped a bandage on the gash that would probably need stiches.

"Car wreck."

"You should change that bandage."

More blood must be showing through. The least of Cooper's worries at the moment. What if he had been wrong, and Hinds was the cartel's snitch? He could have—

Three quick beeps interrupted his spiraling thoughts.

Baker took his cell from his pocket. "Go."

Cooper watched as Baker listened to someone on the other end of the call.

The agent's jaw tightened. "Got it." He lowered his phone. Met Cooper's gaze. "Hinds is dead. Shot."

A rock sank in Cooper's stomach. "When?"

"They're guessing three hours. He was shot in the SUV. They can't find Wentworth."

"The agent with him?"

Baker nodded.

"What do you know about him?"

"Wentworth?" Baker pocketed his phone, hiking his shoulders before letting them drop. "Been an agent about three years, I think. He transferred from an international post. Not sure which country." Lines crossed Baker's forehead. "You don't think—"

"Lance knew there was a leak in the DEA. Somewhere close enough to blow his cover."

Baker's eyes widened.

"Looks like Wentworth is our guy." But that didn't help now. Wouldn't help them find Valena and the twins before—

The possibilities squeezed his chest, crushing his ribs inward. He stepped over to a chair, gripping the back to hold himself up. They could be with the cartel right now. He'd seen the cartel's victims when they were done with them.

Images of bodies that told the wretched tales flashed through his mind, surging vomit up his throat. That could not happen to Valena, the children.

Please, God. Please guide me to them. If it's your will, save them. You know I love them.

Emotion swelled in his chest until he thought he couldn't breathe. He did love them. He hadn't meant to let it happen, but he loved Valena more than he'd ever loved any woman. And he couldn't imagine feeling more affection for children of his own than he felt for Sammy and Savannah. But he could lose them all.

"Cooper?"

He barely heard Baker say his name as his mind and heart battled despair.

When you pass through the waters, I will be with you…

The snippet of the memorized Bible verse cut through his fear. What was the rest of it?

When you walk through fire, you shall not be burned…Fear not, for I am with you.

Peace washed over Cooper, slowing his heart rate and calming his racing mind. God was there, in that moment. He was watching over Valena, Sammy, and Savannah. He hadn't gone anywhere, and He wouldn't. He was in complete control. He would be Cooper's strength and protection for Valena and the twins, no matter what happened.

"Cooper, do you think they're with the cartel?"

He turned around to face Baker, drawing in a deep breath. "Yes."

"It doesn't make sense. The kids aren't worth anything to

them now that Lance is dead. Whatever he had on them died with him."

"We have evidence that will blow them out of the country. We've got the head of their money-laundering operation, and we can prove it."

Baker's eyebrows lifted. "If you give me the evidence, I can take it in, and we can start making arrests."

Cooper held up a hand. "Not so fast. You and the other agents help me get Valena and the twins back, safe, and I'll hand in the evidence myself."

"You have it on you?"

"Do we have a deal?" Cooper met Baker's gaze with an unblinking stare.

"There's no guarantee we can find the hostages in time. What then?"

"We'll find them." Cooper steeled his jaw.

"How?"

"I'm the mouse." Cooper pulled his cell out of his pocket and started a text to Valena's phone. "I just need to ask them where they've set the mousetrap." And pray like he'd never prayed before that God would go with him into the fire.

CHAPTER
TWENTY-NINE

THE DARKNESS CLOAKED VALENA, suffocating her more than the small box she was trapped in. It pressed in on all sides. She'd waited for her eyes to adjust, but black darkness was still all she could see.

How long had she been in there? It felt like hours, but she suspected less time had actually passed. She wasn't sure of anything anymore.

She couldn't quite keep ahold of where she was. Her mind kept drifting back to the moment she'd spent a lifetime trying to forget.

A moldy, stale odor assaulted her nostrils. The smell of the closet.

Panic closed her throat. She was there again. In the closet. Trapped.

The scratchy wool coat brushed her cheek.

She jerked away, lifting her hand to push the coat back. Only air met her fingers.

She shook her head, ignoring the pain as her headache worsened. She was losing her mind.

Hadn't she read somewhere that people who were suffocating could get confused?

She shifted her legs in front of her, the sound of broken glass—the remains of the light fixture—like grit under her shoes, taking her back to that horrible memory.

Sand and grit had stuck to her palms as she'd shoved the shoes aside to crawl to the closet door. Then something had moved under her fingers. A spider?

Her heart had raced as she tried to stamp down her fear. She had to get out for her brother and sister. They were only little kids. Would they be safe while she was trapped?

She threw her ten-year-old body into the door, but it wouldn't budge. How had it gotten locked? Panic churned her stomach and sent a tremor through her. She backed against the coats, covering her mouth with her hands to stop a scream.

Dad would be there soon. She couldn't let him hear her scream. She could just see the look he would give her.

So different than the happy smile she had planned to bring to his face. He was supposed to come home and open the closet to put his boots inside like he always did. And she would be waiting to surprise him and give him a big hug.

But she hadn't known the door was locked when she closed it. And that there was no handle on the inside.

Dad should be there any minute. Her mom had said he was coming home when she'd left to go to mass.

Valena waited, sure he would come.

But the crawling, choking, gnawing fear grew in the darkness. It closed in around her as if making the space to breathe and survive smaller and smaller until she felt crushed by the sheer blackness of it...and the growing certainty that her dad wasn't going to come.

That he never would.

And he hadn't.

Valena pressed her hands to her head as the ache grew. She pushed to her feet, keeping her hands against the cool wall of the safe to orient herself. The door should be to her left.

She tried to keep her mind in the present. She was in a safe, not the closet at that dreadful Army base. She was a grown woman who didn't need her dad.

She would stay awake this time. In the closet, she'd fallen into a fitful sleep until her mother had arrived home, hours later. Her mother had let her out and held her as she sobbed. Her dad hadn't come home that night at all. He'd been called away again.

Valena put out her hand, feeling for the door on the left wall. She caught only air.

Her heart dropped.

She took in a breath through her nose, fighting to stay calm. Must be farther from the entrance than she'd thought. She turned toward the wall she still touched, put both hands on it, and slid toward where she should meet the other wall.

It was up to her to get out of this. No one would come to rescue her this time. Not even Cooper.

Something in her chest torqued painfully. She'd thought he was different from her dad. He cared about the twins, that was obvious. She'd never seen a man be so gentle and interactive with two-year-olds. He treated them as if they were his own. As if he'd be an amazing father.

And he had always come to her aid every step of the way since that night he saved them in Florida.

But he couldn't come this time. Her stomach clenched at the memory of the blood in the car. He was badly injured. Or worse.

And even if he was somehow well, he might not come. He might take the evidence they'd gotten to the DEA first, now that the leak had been exposed. He'd made his choice clear. The DEA had won, and she'd lost.

He really was like her dad. A government job, the thrill of

adventure and a cause always came over family. She couldn't rely on Cooper now or ever.

Her hands reached the corner where the two walls met. She slid her fingers along the other wall. It felt the same.

No door.

Had she gotten turned around?

Panic squeezed her. She couldn't breathe.

But she had to. She had to get to the twins. What was going to happen to them?

She saw the image of their faces, covered in tears the last time she'd seen them. Maybe the last time she would ever see them.

Pain seared her heart as she smacked the wall with her hand. A sob escaped. Then another.

She sank to the floor, her back against the wall as sobs wracked her body.

"God, please help." The plea came out like an involuntary cry she couldn't stop. She dropped her head into her trembling hands, tears soaking her palms.

Is this how her mother had felt? So desperate and alone that she turned to God as her last option? But all her candle-lighting and praying had never done any good.

"God doesn't need good behavior or candle-lighting to please Him or to get Him to do things."

The memory of Cooper's voice, his passion as he'd tried to get her to understand, tugged at her breaking heart. What else had he said? That God offers salvation to anyone who asks.

"God always comes to the rescue, but it's not always the way we expect."

She needed to be rescued. The children needed it, too.

"God," she drew in a shaky breath as her body shuddered on a receding sob, "please save the twins. Cooper says you don't always rescue people the way we want, but Savannah and Sammy are too young to die. To suffer. Please spare them that. Please," more tears spilled from her eyes, "send Cooper to save them."

Like her mom had saved her. Valena lifted her head as realization dawned like a light in her soul.

Cooper was right. God had come to her rescue all those years ago, that horrible night in the closet. He'd sent her mother to get her out. The same mother who had loved and cared for Valena for her whole childhood.

She just hadn't been Valena's dad, the savior she'd been looking for. But her mom had been better, saving her from the darkness of the closet and the greater darkness that would have shrouded her childhood had her mother not been there, loving her through it all.

"Thank you." Valena wiped the tears from her cheeks as her heart pounded. "I'm sorry I didn't see...I didn't..." A fresh wave of emotion sent more moisture to her eyes. "Thank you for your mercy. I know I could die today. I'm probably going to. But I don't want to die denying You. Please, have mercy on me now, too. I'm sorry I've tried to live my life without You. I know I've done so many wrong things. Please forgive me. Please save me."

She bit her lip, tasting salty tears. "Cooper says you're the loving Father I've always wanted. Would you please be my Father? Take me to heaven with You if it's my time to go."

She laid her pounding head back against the wall. Slowly, her trembling stopped, her heart rate slowed, and her breathing evened. She closed her eyes. Her limbs, her whole body felt tired and weak, so very weak.

She opened her eyes, maybe for the last time.

Darkness greeted her. And she wasn't afraid.

Was this what being rescued felt like? Her cold body warmed with the answer. This was what God's rescue felt like.

She even imagined she could see light in the distance. Could this be death?

Her gaze latched on to the sliver of light. Would it grow larger as she drifted away, to heaven? Peace and hope filled her at the thought.

But the sliver stayed the same.

She lifted her head away from the wall, renewing the pounding of her crushing headache. But she narrowed her eyes at the light. Was it real? In the safe?

She got to her feet and moved closer.

The light was coming from just above the floor—a tiny, vertical slash of white. Could it be by the door?

She touched above the light, her fingers running over a surface that felt different, like the edge of a door. She moved both hands to what she hoped was the center of the door and pushed.

It opened.

Impossible. For anyone but God.

A shiver passed through her body, but not from the cold.

Was the door lock on a timer, set to open at this time? Or maybe Wentworth hadn't closed it all the way, and she hadn't noticed? Whatever the explanation, she knew the real reason behind it. God.

Thank you. The simple words—offered as a silent prayer—could never be enough. But, like Cooper had said, they didn't have to be. God had given her this gift, this chance of a new life with Him as her Father. And a chance to save the twins. She wouldn't waste it.

She pushed the door farther open and stepped out of the darkness.

MOVEMENT behind the windows of the office caught Cooper's eye. He signaled to Baker, who ducked behind a large crate.

Cooper made it to the wall of the office and crouched under the windows at the corner. Peered around to see the doorway.

Soft footsteps approached.

A woman with wavy chestnut hair stepped halfway out.

Valena?

His heart lurched into his throat as he stood. "Valena."

She startled, her gaze colliding with his.

Then her smile blinded him.

She threw herself into his arms, and he hugged her back, trying to keep from crushing her against him.

She was alive. He never wanted to let her go.

"You're alive." She pulled her head away from his shoulder as she echoed his thoughts. "Thank God." Those gorgeous violet eyes nearly made him miss what she said.

He lifted his eyebrows.

She nodded. "I prayed when I was in there." She laid her

hand on his chest, shooting a warm pulse through his system. "You were right. God always comes to the rescue."

Cooper smiled as he read the whole story, the change, in her eyes. God had brought her to Him. Cooper's heart skipped a beat. *Thank you, Father.*

"I still can't believe it." She turned her head to glance into the office, where Baker was checking things out. "He opened the door somehow."

"What door?"

"The safe."

Cooper's stomach contorted. "You were in the safe?"

"That's where they left me when they realized you had the flash drive. They were going to use the twins—" She stepped out of his arms, looking around. "Where are the twins? You rescued them, didn't you?"

Alarm cinched his chest. "We just got here. We had the DEA track your phone when the cartel used it to answer my text. They set up an exchange for the flash drive."

She met his gaze, worry swirling in hers.

"We came here first because I hoped they might have left you and the twins behind. They're supposed to give me the twins in exchange for the flash drive, but...we both know that's not what they'll do."

She moved closer and gripped his arms, her face turning white. "We have to get them back."

"Well," Baker stepped out of the office, holding up Valena's cell in his hand, "phone's here and she's here." He nodded to her. "But no kids or bad guys."

Valena jumped her frightened gaze from Baker to Cooper. "We have to—"

"Hey." Cooper touched her shoulder. "We'll get them back."

"How?"

He wished he knew. At the moment, all he knew was that failure was not an option.

Valena tried to focus as Baker and Cooper discussed their strategy for the exchange. All she could think about was the twins, alone with killers. And how slowly Baker seemed to be driving.

A touch on her hand brought her gaze to Cooper, sitting next to her on the bench seat in the back of the SUV.

His warm hand covered hers on the seat between them. "We'll get them back." The confidence in his tone and steadiness of his gaze slowed her heart rate.

She turned her hand up and laced her fingers through his, drawing comfort from the feel of his strength.

His eyes darkened. "I thought I might have lost you. When I heard the cartel had taken you..." He ran his tongue over his lips and drew in a breath that sounded shaky. His gaze dropped to their joined hands.

Her pulse tripped. "I thought I might have lost you, too." Her voice was thick with emotion she tried to hold back. But she'd done that enough. She let the tears drop to her cheeks.

Cooper looked up, hitting her with those rich brown eyes she loved. He reached a thumb to her face and wiped away her tears.

She closed her eyes at his achingly gentle touch.

"I don't know how things will go down at the exchange, so I want to say this now. I love you, Valena."

Her eyes popped open as her breath whooshed from her lungs, then returned in a rush to fuel her sprinting heart. She looked into the deep passion reflected in his eyes. "I love you, too, Cooper White." She placed her free hand on his handsome jawline. "And I trust you."

He reached up to take that hand in his, too. He turned it over and pressed a kiss into her palm.

A shiver shot from her hand through her arm. If things were different, she knew she'd see a smile and maybe get the full-on kiss she'd been waiting for. But part of her heart was missing as long as her babies were in jeopardy.

The concern in Cooper's eyes and the tension around his mouth verified he felt the same.

They had to get them back.

She took in a breath. "How are we going to rescue them?"

"Do you really know how to use a gun?"

She sat up straighter and cocked an eyebrow. "I'm a better shot than my dad."

"Ever use a rifle?"

"Which model? I prefer the AR-15 myself."

The corner of Cooper's lips twitched. "You're hired."

The second of amusement was quickly squelched by the anxiety that churned her stomach. "Will this work?"

His jaw tightened. "We're outnumbered and outgunned. But I'm praying like mad that God will show up."

VALENA LEANED out to look over the edge of the parking garage roof. A cold updraft gusted from below, slapping her face. Good thing she'd never been afraid of heights.

The street lay so far away, dotted with lights that reflected off the snow. The headlights of a plow cut two V's in the darkness as the big truck left blacktop peeking through white in its wake.

"Ready?"

She stepped back and turned to Baker.

"Better double-check the knot."

She tugged on the knot that secured the rope around and underneath her legs and waist, forming a seat that would hold her as Baker lowered her off the roof.

"Nervous?"

She took the AR-15 Baker extended toward her and brought the sling over her head, letting the rifle hang against her back. She met his gaze. "Determined."

A slight smile angled the agent's mouth. "You and Cooper make a good team."

"Let's hope so." Adrenaline flowed into her system, building energy in her core. She might have to jump off the side and go for the twins herself if Cooper didn't text in the next few seconds.

God, please protect my babies.

Were they crying? Being mistreated?

She turned to face the drop below, pushing away the fear. God was watching over them.

They should be right down there, on the third level of the parking garage where the cartel told Cooper to meet them alone.

The twins were probably in the cartel's SUV, alive and unharmed in the expectation that Cooper would demand to see them before handing over the flash drive. At least that's what Valena and Cooper hoped.

"That's it."

She twisted her head to see Baker look up from his cell, her movement causing a surge of the headache that had mostly drifted to the background.

"He's going in."

"Okay." She swung one leg over the short concrete wall, sitting on it as she glanced at Baker. "I'm ready."

He grabbed the rope slack and braced himself, pulling back until she felt the resistance. "Go."

She leaned forward and held onto the wall with her hands as she lowered both legs over the side.

"Ready." Baker's almost-whisper reached her ears.

She took a breath and transferred her hands to the rope. "Go."

He began to slowly lower her.

She pushed slightly off the wall with her feet like she'd seen people do in the movies. Maybe she shouldn't have refused to go wall-climbing with her dad when he'd wanted to teach her yet another adventure skill.

He hadn't given her a choice about instructing her how to shoot and handle different guns. For the first time in her life, she was glad. His insistence on pounding tactics and combat strategy into her head was about to come in handy, too.

She looked down, the street moving slightly closer but still a far enough drop she wouldn't want Baker to lose his grip.

She counted the levels as she passed them, each one silent and dark, spattered with only a few cars at two o'clock in the morning. She pulled out her phone from her jacket pocket as she neared what should be the fourth level from the bottom.

Punching in a text to Baker, she returned the phone to her pocket and brought her other hand to the rope.

She stopped, slightly above the dark opening between the floor and ceiling of the fifth and fourth levels. She let go with one hand to whip out her phone again.

Five more feet.

A few seconds. Then the rope lowered, too slow for her racing heartbeat.

The wall of the fourth level was just below. She looked down, aiming to land her legs on top of it as Baker lowered her.

A gust of wind swung her body away instead.

He kept lowering.

She might miss it.

She swung her legs toward the wall. The movement brought her closer.

Reaching with her arms, she grabbed the wall. She pulled her body up and over and brought her feet inside to the solid ground of the parking level.

The rope went slack as Baker continued to lower.

She tugged it hard, twice.

It stopped.

She loosened the makeshift harness and stepped out of the rope as fast as she could, her pulse sprinting double-time. She'd taken too long. She could've gone in before Cooper to already be in position. But he had insisted she wait so the cartel's attention would be on him when she snuck down to the third level.

She dropped the rope and pulled the AR-15 over her head to have it ready as she quietly made her way down the sloped ramps to the third level.

Her heart clenched. She'd better be in time to make sure that attention didn't get Cooper killed.

Darkness waited for Cooper as he gripped his weapon and slowly walked down the ramp from the elevator to the lower portion of the third level. He let his footsteps echo, hoping to mask any sound from Valena.

Had she made it down okay?

He pushed aside the worry. He needed to have faith in her and God. And Baker. *Father, you know we need you now more than ever. Make this work. Protect Valena and the twins.*

He rounded the pillar that had two cars parked on either side of it.

Headlights popped on, shining in his face.

He quickly stepped to the side of the direct beams.

The cartel's SUV was responsible for the headlights, facing him at the end of the aisle before the next turn.

Wulford's sports car was parked with ironic orderliness in an angled stall halfway between Cooper and the SUV.

Good. She'd come herself.

The woman stepped out in front of the headlights, two thugs with AR-15's flanking her. "Mr. White. We meet at last." The empty space carried her voice to him with an echo.

"Can't say it's a pleasure."

"Likewise." She folded her arms across her suit jacket. "You have the flash drive?"

"You have the children?"

She lifted a hand, silhouetted by the headlights, and tipped two fingers.

The side door of the SUV opened.

He forced his breathing to stay calm, his gaze to take in everything instead of laser-focusing on that door. But his gut seized when a man emerged, holding Sammy and Savannah, one on each arm.

He couldn't see them well in the darkness, but what he could see made his blood boil. "You didn't have to gag them."

"Children are horrifically noisy, don't you think?" Wulford flicked her hand, and the thug moved like he was going to return the twins to the SUV.

"Hold it." Cooper pushed a commanding tone into his voice.

The man paused.

"I need to make sure they're all right."

"You can see they're alive." Wulford took one step forward. "If you want them to stay that way, you'll give us the flash drive. Drop it on the ground and back away."

"Not until I know the children are okay. That they can stand and walk."

Silence as Wulford stared at him.

Then she lifted her hand. "Put them down, but do not let them go."

Cooper's muscles twitched as the guy lowered the children to stand on their feet, keeping his big hands clamped on their tiny arms.

Lord, please let Valena be ready. And let her be as good a shot as she said.

"Have you seen enough?" The Wulford woman's voice held an edge of superiority he hoped she was about to lose.

His nerves tingled as he waited. "Plenty." He tightened his grip on his Glock.

A shot burst through the garage.

CHAPTER
THIRTY-TWO

THE BIG GUY with the twins shrieked, clutching the leg Valena had shot while Carissa Wulford ran for cover on the other side of the SUV.

The cartel thugs opened fire as they crouched around the vehicle.

Valena ducked behind the half wall that had given her a perfectly elevated position above the third level's lower section.

Another gun fired. Cooper.

She peeked over the wall.

He was answering the barrage with his Glock, using Carissa's sports car for cover.

The twins stood beside the fallen man, their eyes big, and their mouths wrapped with awful gags.

Where was Baker?

Tires squealed, accompanied by the sound of an engine beneath her.

Baker.

They needed to keep the cartel busy. She fired at the headlights of the cartel's SUV, taking out one, then the other as Cooper let off another round.

She ducked as return bullets whizzed too close to her head.

"He's getting the kids!" a man shouted.

She popped up to look.

Baker swept the twins into his arms.

A cartel man moved toward them.

She aimed—

Cooper's Glock went off.

The man yelled, dropping his gun as he grabbed his arm. He crawled into the back of the SUV through the still-open door.

The sound of an engine gunning below signaled Baker was leaving. With the twins. They were safe.

Thank you, God.

Relief cascaded through her limbs. Her heart screamed at her to drop the rifle and run out of there to hold her babies in her arms. But Cooper wasn't safe yet. And neither was she.

They had to end this.

"Drop it."

She froze at the deep voice behind her.

"Put down the rifle. Easy."

She slowly lowered the weapon to the floor and stood.

The chair sitter from the factory aimed a gun at her, his tense jaw and unblinking stare showing her marksmanship had at least gained her some respect. "I've got her!" His yell echoed through the garage. "Move." He stepped back and angled his body to indicate she should head for the lower level via the ramp.

"Mr. White? Did you hear that?" Carissa's question carried a note of triumph.

Valena walked a few feet in front of the man, her stomach twisting as her pulse pounded in her ears.

The thug must have come up on the elevator in the corner. How could she have been so stupid as to leave herself vulnerable to attack from behind? She should've paid more attention to her dad's lectures on tactics.

But she hadn't. And now Cooper might pay for it, too. *Please, God, don't let him get hurt.*

She reached the turn marked by a thick pillar.

"Hold it." Her captor came up closer behind her. "I'll shoot you if he tries anything. Now move. Slowly."

She rounded the corner in the middle of the ramp.

Cooper, crouched by the sports car, still held his gun.

"Drop it, White. Or she gets it right now."

Valena's heart lodged in her throat. She wanted to tell him not to listen. To just shoot the man even if it got her killed. At least Cooper might get away alive.

But she knew the man she trusted would never do that. She'd seen it in his eyes when he'd found her, alive, at the factory. She'd seen it in everything he'd said and done since the first time he'd rescued her.

She saw it in the intense gaze he locked on her now as he stood and lowered his gun.

He wouldn't leave her. No matter what it cost him.

Renewed strength filled her limbs. She couldn't let him die for her.

"Drop the gun."

Cooper set his Glock on the hood of the car.

Valena glanced back to gauge the distance between herself and the man giving orders behind her. He wasn't close enough. She'd have to change that.

"Come over here, Mr. White." Carissa came out of hiding and stood at the front of the SUV in a wide stance that stretched her skirt across her slim frame.

Cooper left his gun and walked around the car to head toward Carissa.

Every muscle yearned for her to go to Cooper as they both neared Carissa and the cartel men that gathered in a staggered line behind her. But Valena's plan would only work if she didn't. So she obeyed her captor when he told her to stop ten feet to the right of Cooper.

"You've lost, Mr. White." Carissa's teeth flashed with her Cheshire grin. "I'll take the flash drive." She extended her hand.

"Sure, I can give you the flash drive." Cooper's calm gaze and cool tone weakened Carissa's smile. "But it won't stop the evidence from getting out through the copy we made."

She glared. "What copy? Who did you give it to?" She practically hissed as she took a step toward him.

"I'm afraid I can't tell you that."

"You're bluffing."

Cooper met her stare head-on. "Are you willing to take that risk?"

"Tell me where the copy is." Her voice pinched.

"Let her go, and I'll tell you."

Valena's stomach plummeted. No. She would never leave him.

Carissa stepped closer to Cooper, her eyes flashing. "Or you can give it to me, and I won't have her shot right now." She flicked her hand at the man behind Valena.

He moved in, grabbed Valena around the neck with one arm and pushed the gun barrel into her head with his other hand.

Her heart crashed against her ribs as adrenaline surged through her veins. This was it.

She met Cooper's worried gaze, shifted hers pointedly to Carissa and back again.

The concern left his eyes as they darkened. He understood.

He looked at Carissa. "You hurt her, and you're finished."

She stepped even closer to him. "Shoot her."

Valena swung up her arm and crashed it into her captor's

elbow. She gripped the gun in his hand as his arm flung out, and she jammed her elbow into his ribs.

Carissa squealed, Cooper probably grabbing her as Valena fought her way out of the man's grip.

Valena spun away as his arm fell off her neck. She kept ahold of the Glock, twisting it around so the man's fingers bent backward on the handle as she braced his wrist in a twisted position between her hand and the gun.

He grimaced in pain, but she knew he could try any number of attacks with her so close. She yanked the gun away and darted back.

The other men stayed near the SUV, their weapons at the ready.

Because Cooper held Carissa in the hold Valena had just been in. His Glock pressed into the side of her head, and his arm wrapped around her neck. "Tell them to stand down."

"Lower your weapons." A tremor broke Carissa's usual strong tone.

The men didn't move as Valena kept the Glock trained on them.

"I'm sorry, Mr. White." A shaky smile shaded Carissa's lips, not touching the stark fear in her eyes. "But I don't think I'll be of much help. I'm afraid my death warrant's already been signed."

"Good. Then you'll be willing to cooperate with the DEA."

"Why not?" Carissa let out a humorless laugh. "If we get out of this alive."

"We will. But they won't." Cooper's stall tactic was working.

None of the men seemed willing to take the first shot and be the first one to take a bullet from Valena.

Now if the DEA would just—

Sirens sounded near the building, then echoed in the garage. Baker had gotten them to come.

Thank you, God. Thank you.

She glanced at Cooper as the cartel men lowered their weapons.

"Bet you never thought you'd be glad to see the DEA." Humor warmed his voice as that grin she loved appeared.

She returned her gaze to the cartel, keeping her gun ready just in case. But the corner of her lips twitched as she shrugged one shoulder. "Depends on the agent."

There was one she'd never get tired of seeing, for better or worse, so long as they both should live.

EPILOGUE

Ten months later. Miami, Florida.

"MY FIRST DADDY?"

Valena set the photo of Lance and Miriam on the end table in the living room and turned toward her girl.

Savannah looked at the picture positioned at her eye-level as she clutched the pink bunny Cooper had given her.

Valena squatted down, looking into those clear blue eyes. "Yes, that's your first daddy." A lump filled her throat, as it always did when she thought of Lance.

If only he could somehow know that he'd accomplished what he'd set out to do. Cooper and Valena had delivered the evidence that ended the cartel's U.S. money laundering and put Carissa Wulford in prison, but Lance's death had driven the nail into the cartel's coffin.

Maybe Lance had done it on purpose, gotten the head of the cartel in Columbia to become personally involved in his murder. It worked. The kingpin made a mistake and left evidence that connected him to Lance's killing. It was enough for Columbian authorities to be able to take down the man they'd wanted to indict for years. Lance had given his life to end the cartel and make his country a safer place for his children.

Valena hadn't realized before how much he'd thought of the twins and their future. He'd left the Florida house to Valena and the cottage in Wisconsin to the children, to be cared for by Valena until they were adults. Money would never be a problem for them either, since Lance and Miriam left plentiful funds for Valena to raise them and trust funds for the twins' future.

The adoption had gone through quickly, making Cooper and Valena the twins' parents, now. But Valena would make sure they grew up knowing that their first father had been a hero. And that he had loved them.

The sound of a door opening made Savannah spin away from the photo as Valena's heart skipped a beat.

"Daddy's home!" Sammy's yell preceded the boy by a split-second as he darted past the living room, his sister running to join him.

A smile stretching her lips, Valena walked at a more adult pace to the hallway where her husband stood, partially through the door from the garage with the twins in his arms.

Cooper's gaze found hers. The heat in his eyes sent a shiver from her head to her toes. "Hey." His lips curved in the special smile he only gave her.

"Hey, yourself." How was it that her heart still raced like a kamikaze every time he looked at her like that?

He gave the twins a bounce. "Guess what Daddy got for you today?"

"What? What?" They spoke practically in unison as they pulled back from clinging to his neck and stared in his face with wide eyes.

"In the bag down there." He lowered them to the floor, shut the door with his foot, and lifted the plastic shopping bag he must have dropped when the twins had rushed him. "Who wants to guess what it is?"

Valena laughed. "Don't torture them."

Cooper grinned and pulled out two flashlights.

"A flash-ight!" Sammy jumped to reach his blue one as Cooper handed it to him.

"A flashlight, Mommy!" Savannah trotted over to Valena, clutching her yellow prize.

"Ooh, it's beautiful, sweetie." Valena crouched to examine the flashlight. "Do you know how it works?"

"I do." Sammy proudly marched over to his sister and showed her how to slide the switch that would turn it on and off.

Valena stood, exchanging an amused look with Cooper.

"I wanna try it in my room." Sammy looked at Valena. "With the lights off. Can I?"

"You may." She smiled as her angels took off for the bedrooms, squealing and chatting about their new presents.

Valena turned to her husband, feigning a frown. "You spoil them far too much."

Cooper closed the distance between them and slid his arms around her waist. "A flashlight is practical."

She smiled at his handsome face, only inches from hers, as her pulse picked up speed. "Very."

"And I wanted to celebrate."

She pulled back slightly in his hold. "Did you get it?"

His eyebrows drew together. "You mean you wanted a present?"

She didn't miss the twinkle in his eyes. "Don't joke about something like this, Mr. White."

"Very well, Mrs. White." He pressed his forehead to hers as his eyes brightened the way they always did when he used her married name. "Yes. I got it."

She squealed like one of the children and threw her arms

around his neck. "I'm so proud of you." Her words were muffled in his shoulder, so she pulled back and said them again. "I'm so very proud of you, Special Agent Cooper White."

He searched her gaze, his mouth in a thoughtful line. "Are you sure this is what you want?"

She couldn't help but trace the chiseled edge of his jaw with her finger. "Is it what you want?"

The passion in his eyes was her answer.

She nodded. "Then it's what I want, too."

"Everything's been cleared, and they gave me the post here in Florida for now." He shifted his arms, cradling her with his hands on her back. "But that doesn't guarantee..." He glanced away, then brought a worried gaze to her face. "DEA is a dangerous job wherever it's done."

"Cooper," she rested her palm on his chest, "I know that. But I also know I trust you and I trust God. Whatever happens, God will be with us." She smiled as her love for this man swelled in her heart till she thought it might burst. "You need to do what God has called you to do."

Cooper's full lips formed her favorite smile. "Because some things should never be sacrificed."

"Exactly."

"Not my wife."

Her smile broadened. "Not my husband."

"Not family." He lowered his head toward hers.

"Not love."

His mouth hovered over hers. "Not this." His whispered breath melded with hers as he claimed her lips in a kiss that would've knocked her socks off if she hadn't been barefoot.

She returned his kiss with equal passion until giggles drifted through the whirl that clouded her senses.

Cooper ended the kiss reluctantly, with a ragged breath, as the twins patted their parents' legs with small hands.

"Mommy." Sammy looked up, tugging on Valena's shorts. "I can eat now?"

Cooper and Valena laughed as Cooper scooped Sammy into his arms. Valena hefted Savannah, and they stole the moment for a family hug.

As Valena basked in the light of their love, her heart whispered her greatest prayer.

Thank you, Father, for rescuing us all.

Turn the Page for a Special Sneak Peek of
WINDY CITY WESTONS, BOOK 1

WAYLAID

AVAILABLE NOW

EXCERPT OF WAYLAID

Chicago. August 28. 9:26 p.m.

A POP PIERCED THE NIGHT.

A gunshot? Spring Weston's stomach clenched as she ducked lower over the handlebars of her bicycle and peddled hard. A shooting wouldn't be a surprise in that neighborhood, but she'd rather avoid a run-in with a stray bullet.

She glanced into the hazy darkness on either side of her as she kept her pace steady, light raindrops mixing with sweat on her face.

Nothing moved in the glow from streetlamps.

A white van waited next to some business with barred windows. The building's sign was a yellow blur as she whizzed by, maintaining her racing speed.

She tapped the backlight on the timer attached to the handlebars. Great pace. Faster than she should be at mile ten. Adrenaline and nerves must be driving her legs.

Drugs. Doping. On *her* team.

The anxiety wadding in her stomach threatened to choke her. She puffed out a breath, willing her muscles to relax as she kept pedaling at the same clip.

She glided through a curve into the headwind. Rain pelted her face.

"Doping? Are you kidding me?" Cliff's denial echoed in her ears, louder than the wind that rushed past. *"I run a clean team. You know that."*

"But I saw Megan...popping pills." Spring had watched her coach, desperately hoping he would offer some explanation she could believe.

"How do you know they were drugs? She takes supplements all the time."

"Megan told me what the pills were."

Cliff laughed. "She told you? That'd be pretty dumb if she was doping, wouldn't it?"

Spring frowned at his jovial grin. "Megan didn't think I'd care. She thought it was expected. She said—" Spring moistened her lips. "She said the whole team is doing it."

"Well, there you go."

Spring raised her eyebrows.

"Obviously, she was just joking. She knows you don't take drugs." Cliff's grin angled sideways. "You know what a kidder Megan is. You gotta learn to lighten up and not take things so seriously."

She stared at him. Why couldn't he be more convincing? Offer some explanation or at least a denial that he was involved?

He had stepped closer to her, his grin softening into a smile that seemed to hide something. "Come on, Spring. Don't you trust me more than that?"

She had trusted him. But she knew what she had seen Megan take, what Megan had said. It wasn't a joke. At least not to Spring.

She shifted her shoulders, trying to relax as she surged through the neighborhood she was moving too fast to see.

The rain weakened, but her tense thoughts pelted her from the inside.

If only it wasn't true. If only she hadn't met Megan for a training run and seen her take those pills.

Spring pressed her lips together, trapping her breath longer than she should. She had no hard evidence to prove doping on the team. Only what Megan had told her. Would anyone believe her if she reported it? She could hardly believe it herself.

But she couldn't knowingly compete on a team that was doping. Every win would mean nothing. And the scandal could come out once she made it to an elite team. Everyone would think she had doped, too.

Lord, give me wisdom. Calm slid through her chest with the prayer, soothing the tension and allowing her to breathe more evenly.

She would have to report what she knew. Whether or not anyone believed her wasn't her responsibility.

Relief flowed to her fingers with the confidence that she'd made the right decision.

Readjusting her position over the handlebars, she focused on pushing her pace back up. A praise song from church started to play in her head, lending a driving beat to her pedaling rhythm.

She sailed into the curve under the overpass, the road wet enough to make her slow just slightly.

She sped into the straightaway.

A rumble behind her.

Ugh. Traffic. Unusual for the area at that time of night.

She drifted closer to the curb to let the driver pass, not slowing her pace.

The rumble grew louder. Why wasn't the car passing?

She glanced back.

A white blur slammed into her bicycle. Catapulted her.

She flew, airborne.

Her breath caught as time stood still.

A concrete abutment waited for her.

She was going to die.

Someone wants to kill her. She wants the killer to finish the job.

Spring Weston will do anything to rise in the ranks of pro cycling and prove she isn't the one failure of the five Weston siblings. Anything except cheat. When she learns of doping on her cycling team, she's determined to uncover the truth. But she can't if she's dead.

Sergeant Torin Cotter may not be the hero the public thinks he is, but he recognizes fear when he sees it. When he takes over the investigation of the collision that landed Spring in the hospital, he's compelled to protect her from whatever danger she's in, even though he knows he might fail. Again.

Spring's faith in God isn't enough to help her face the living nightmare she awakened to after the accident. But neither she nor the handsome sergeant see the greater threat that's coming until it's too late.

If they're going to survive, Spring and Torin will not only have to confront their worst fears—they'll have to find a reason to live.

Shop *Waylaid* at JerushaAgen.com

She never invites visitors. But visitors sometimes invite themselves.

When a winter storm brings more than snow, May Denver is forced to flee from her home and fight for her life. Can she trust an unwanted neighbor and risk her greatest fear in order to survive?

GRAB THIS ROMANTIC SUSPENSE STORY FOR FREE WHEN YOU SIGN UP FOR JERUSHA'S NEWSLETTER

www.FearWarriorSuspense.com

GUARDIANS UNLEASHED
"Fast-paced suspense at its best."
- DiAnn Mills, bestselling author of Concrete Evidence
JERUSHA AGEN
RISING DANGER
JERUSHA AGEN
HIDDEN DANGER
JERUSHA AGEN
COVERT DANGER
JERUSHA AGEN
UNSEEN DANGER
JERUSHA AGEN
LETHAL DANGER
JERUSHA AGEN
TERMINAL DANGER
GuardiansUnleashed.com

ABOUT JERUSHA

Jerusha Agen imagines danger around every corner but knows God is there, too. So naturally, she writes romantic suspense infused with the hope of salvation in Jesus Christ.

Jerusha loves to hang out with her big furry dogs and little furry cats, often while reading or watching movies.

Find more of Jerusha's thrilling, fear-fighting stories at www.JerushaAgen.com.

facebook.com/JerushaAgenAuthor

instagram.com/jerushaagen